OLIVE
AND
MARY ANNE

James T. Farrell

Stonehill Publishing Company

ISBN: 0-88373-071-5
Library of Congress Catalog Card Number: 77-081172

Illustrations by Joseph Graham.

Book design by Heather White.

First printing.

Printed in U.S.A.

CONTENTS

OLIVE AND AND MARY ANNE

[OLIVE ARMSBURG]

ONE

Olive Armsburg came to see Eddie Ryan, uninvited. She brought a bottle even though she knew he didn't drink. She had several. He found himself thinking that it was only a matter of time before she would be committed again. Poor Olive. She has been institutionalized three times and received shock treatments every time.

When Eddie met her twenty years ago, Olive Armsburg Jameson had been a quiet, rather pretty girl, with red hair. But even then there was very little expression in her face. There was, however, a delicacy, a delicacy that is gone now. She was married to Mortimer Jameson at the time. Their son, Roy, went to the same school as Eddie's son, Tommy. Olive had read several of Eddie's early books and talked about them intelligently. She wanted to paint. She showed Ryan some of her work; she did have talent. Her husband was a businessman with no other real interest. Olive's parents were very rich and were glad to help their son-in-law on his way up. Olive was an only child.

Olive had been a shy girl, an almost pretty heiress. But she hadn't wanted to be Olive Armsburg, the heiress. She wanted to be Olive Armsburg, the artist. Instead, she had married. But she still longed to paint. Mortimer Jameson didn't object. A woman had to do something with her time and painting was as good a hobby as any.

Mortimer Jameson was anything but sensitive. There was neither profit nor loss in being sensitive, which, to Mortimer, meant there was no reason for it.

When Eddie Ryan met them, there were no signs of a breakup, but their mutual disappointment did surface occasionally. Olive was not impressed with the money Mortimer made. Her father had made much more. Whenever Mortimer tried to discuss business transactions with her, she would shut off his voice. She resented his attitude that his business was more important than her painting. Olive had other resentments. She began to brood. To avoid despair, she would will her mind blank and try to black out the world around her.

As time went on, Olive began to will these blank spells more frequently.

They were both disappointed in their marriage but there was their son, Roy. They had to think about him.

Mortimer, at times, would pose as a reasonable, practical, and considerate husband. But he did not love Olive. Who could love her now? He didn't know what was the matter with her. Going home at night was like going—he didn't know what to call it. There was no pleasure in it for him and a man was entitled to pleasure at the end of a working day.

It was Olive who suggested they move in with her parents. Her parents' Park Avenue apartment was so big that there would be no problem about crowding each other. Olive had asked her mother if it would be all right. Hannah Armsburg welcomed the idea. Olive's father was less enthusiastic.

He was past sixty and he had worked hard all his life. His family had gained from his hard work. It was time to think of himself now. He wasn't going to live forever. For many, life was a bad bargain. He didn't want it to be for him. He wanted to show a profit, not sustain a loss. He was a millionaire. He had accomplished the dreams and ambitions of his youth. And he had gotten smarter, shrewder, and more sure of himself. But he paid a high price for this. He paid with Time.

He was going to stick out the marriage. This is what Mortimer Jameson decided. Sure he could make his own pile but Olive's father had made a bigger pile, and two piles were better than one. Besides, it would be a headache—trouble and expense—to break up with Olive. Yes, he would stick it out. Other men did and managed to have fun on the side. He and Olive could go along as they had. And now that they were living with her parents, he didn't have to be alone with her so much. From time to time, if he had to, he would find fun and relaxation elsewhere.

Olive Armsburg had never been told that she would one day be a millionaire but she had absorbed it. She had grown up surrounded by rich and powerful men. The strongest influence on her had been that of her father. But there were others: her grandfather Gustav Armsburg and her uncle Moe Armsburg. All three men had been determined to become millionaires and they had. They treated Olive as a special little girl. They were too busy making money to give her time but they bought her presents. Olive liked getting them. Presents made her feel loved. Money was connected with love.

As Olive grew up, more and more money was spent on her so that she would be loved. There was money for dancing schools, for music lessons, for braces, and for clothes.

Olive came to understand what was expected of her. She would marry a well-to-do young man, preferably a German Jew, with good prospects.

Olive had had a few crushes on boys but she wanted love. Love was something wonderful, something that would make her happy. It would change her life but it would not change her. It would bring out the real Olive in her.

Olive Armsburg met Mortimer Jameson at a party. She was twenty-four; he was twenty-six. The party was held in a big apartment on Central Park West by Diana Nathanson. Olive had changed her mind about going several times but finally she decided to go. There she met Mortimer Jameson.

It was not until after the marriage that Olive learned that Mortimer's name had been Mortimer Julianson. He had changed it legally to Jameson. This did not trouble her. She heard her father say: "If Jameson is a better name to use in getting ahead, what sense would there be for Mortimer to go on calling himself Julianson?"

Another time he said: "Julianson by the name of Jameson is just so much more business. In a nutshell, it's good business."

Julianson or Jameson. She was a Mrs. now. She was a woman now the way her mother and father wanted her to be. They hadn't rushed her. She was twenty-four. She'd had the music and the lights, the parties and the dancing, the kisses in the moonlight. She'd been held and hugged and kissed. There had been boat trips, dancing on boats, warm spring nights in Central Park. It was time for her to be married.

TWO

Both Mortimer and Olive considered living with her parents a temporary arrangement. They knew that eventually they would have to establish their own home but neither of them looked forward to this. They regarded it an obligation. Olive particularly felt this. She was a married woman now, not a girl to be living at home. And yet, this was still strange to her. How could it have happened? Why? It was a puzzle. She had no answer to these questions.

But that was silly. She knew how it had happened.

Olive had been a virgin when she married Mortimer but she'd heard that something wonderful, so wonderful that you couldn't describe it, happened to you. Nothing wonderful happened to her.

She didn't even want to remember the first time. She and Mortimer had gotten on the train at Pennsylvania Station. Her father and mother waved at them from the platform. Others from the wedding were there. Finally the train started.

Once in their own compartment, Mortimer couldn't wait. And even though it was early afternoon and she wished that he could wait, she hadn't said anything. She wished it had been darker. She didn't like taking off her clothes in front of a man, even if the man was her husband. But she did it. It was awful. She had no privacy once she stood naked before him.

It hurt.

She wished he would get on top of her again. She wanted to feel something besides hurting. The train was moving. She turned her head toward the wall. Mortimer was on top of her again. She was waiting for love to come.

Love did not come.

It happened again sometime in the night.

The train was going fast and the Pullman car shook. Nothing happened that time either.

When Olive awakened on the train the next morning, she was frightened. The loss of her virginity troubled her. Mortimer tried to talk to her. He wanted to know how it felt, if she had felt him inside her. His questions embarrassed her. She felt an overwhelming loneliness as she stared out the train window.

Later, at breakfast, Mortimer tried again to talk to her. But Olive could not speak. Mortimer knew that something was wrong. Olive wasn't acting the way she ought to be. She was his wife but she was not acting the way a wife should act. He didn't know what to think. What was going on in that pretty head? She was pretty, he thought, looking at her. Was she as pretty as she had been yesterday?

Well, he wouldn't worry about it now. It was not the time nor the place.

They ate their breakfast.

Mortimer and Olive returned to their Pullman car room. The porter had made up the bed. They sat, staring through the window. Mortimer wished they were already in Miami.

"Florida," Olive said.

"What about Florida, Olive?"

He had wanted to say "dear" but couldn't.

"Oh nothing."

"You've never been to Florida before, Olive?"

"No."

This had surprised him when she first told him. With all of her father's money, he thought it odd that she had never been there.

Olive was watching him. Mortimer Jameson was her husband. She was trying to make the thought stick so she could believe it. Or accept it. That was what she meant. Accept it. She did believe it.

The train was grinding along, past earth burned by the sun, past houses whose once bright colors had been faded by that same sun.

What was the matter with her?
Olive asked herself this question.
Mortimer, watching her unhappy face, asked himself: What is the matter with her?

The train kept starting and stopping, starting and stopping, with much jerking and banging of cars. Time passed slowly.
God, what a boring day, Olive thought. But it wasn't Mortimer's fault. It was the train ride. That was it. The train. Once they got off, everything would be different.
Should she have married Mortimer Jameson?
The question frightened her. She couldn't walk out now. People would think she was crazy. They would say she hadn't given the marriage a chance. That was what honeymoons were for. They gave young people a chance to know each other. Once she and Mortimer were relaxed and on the beach, everything would be all right.

The sun was warm. She liked the sun. It made you feel drugged and sleepy. It made you forget.
There were many other people from New York at the hotel. Olive was shier than usual. She was ashamed, too. It had not happened yet. She didn't like to say the word but she would say it to herself. Orgasm. She had not had an orgasm.
"You're a newlywed, aren't you, dear?"
A woman in the hotel lobby spoke to Olive. She was in her thirties, with dark hair and a round plump face. Bright red lipstick made her full lips look thicker.
"I saw you when you came in with your husband."
Olive tried to smile at her.
"My name is Rothenberg. Selma Rothenberg."
"How do you do, Mrs. Rothenberg."
"Call me Selma, dear."
Olive smiled.

"You're a sweet little thing," Selma Rothenberg said.

Olive looked at her. Did this woman know she was rich?

"Let's go sit in the lobby for a while."

Olive followed the woman to a nearby couch. Maybe she shouldn't be doing this. But why not if she wanted to? She was a full-grown married woman now.

The thought struck her.

Olive scarcely heard Selma Rothenberg. For the first time since she had married Mortimer Jameson a few days ago, she felt like herself. She felt like Olive Armsburg, not like Mrs. Mortimer Jameson. Until she saw Mortimer again, she could be free. She wouldn't have to mind her P's and Q's. With him, she had to be careful, even about the smallest matters. She wasn't sure why she felt this way, but she did. It was for her own good.

THREE

Olive grew up believing that only successful men were of any account. If they weren't successful, there was something wrong with them. She was well into her teens before she questioned this. Then she decided that it was foolish and wondered why so many people, her father among them, believed anything so silly.

But even though Olive laughed at this notion, she had not completely dismissed it. Neither had she questioned her father or her grandfather on this. She hadn't asked them aloud. But that didn't matter, she'd asked them in her own mind. There should be a sign for minds to keep off the grass. Keep your mind off the grass. She had to laugh at this.

She shouldn't think about things like this. And if she couldn't make herself think about other things, then she'd have to not think about anything. She'd have to make her mind go blank. She could do that. Sometimes when she did, she felt something strange happen to her. She felt that she couldn't talk, couldn't say what she wanted to say. It was the same as dreaming, the same as when you dream you're walking and not moving. She would be moving inside herself and the air would be moving just like she was moving inside herself. There was movement, moving inside her, in her legs, in her arms, even up in her head. Everything would get strange. She would know where she was and she would recognize things but everything would seem strange. And she would seem strange, too.

Olive did not tell anybody when this happened to her. They might say there was something wrong with her in the head. Maybe there was, but what was going on in her head was better than what was going on around her. When she was little, she had deliberately dreamed up moods. Whenever she had been lonely or sad, she would slip into her bedroom and daydream there in the dark. But she had to be more careful now. She was married. She couldn't go off whenever she wanted to and daydream. Mortimer would think she was peculiar. He was too much of a businessman to spend time daydreaming.

Olive didn't want to believe that her periods of blankness were beyond her control. That would mean something was the matter with her. If only she could talk to someone. Mortimer. Her mother. That's what husbands were for. And mothers. But Olive was afraid.

The fear that something was the matter with her was in back of her mind. What she meant by "something the matter" was "crazy." Olive was afraid she might be crazy. The thought terrified her. And her panic made things worse. She did not remember things she should remember. She began having depressive moods. She rarely spoke, afraid she would reveal something that would make others suspicious.

Olive's parents had noticed that there was something wrong with their daughter. And Mortimer knew there was something wrong. He didn't know what it was exactly, but he did know that it got on his nerves. The way she sat, not saying anything, with that blank look on her face. He certainly hadn't bargained for this kind of wife. He had gotten some deal, all right. Here he was, a man on the way up, married to a crackpot. Well, no one could blame him for her condition. He had done nothing to cause this. She must have been this way before he married her. But there were people, of course, who would claim that she was fine until she married him.

It was important to Mortimer Jameson what people thought.

Mortimer blamed her. This didn't surprise her. She had known that he would. Yes, she had known. What had she known? She couldn't remember. But she knew that she had known what she had known. She was a little bit crazy. No she wasn't. She was only imagining again. That was what it was, imagining. She was perfectly all right. She would just have to be careful. She must not let other people suspect about her imagination. She would have to hide it from everybody. If no one else knew, she would be all right. She wasn't crazy; she knew who she was. Her name was Olive. Olive Armsburg Jameson. Or maybe Julianson. What was inside the big round "O" that was the first letter of her name? That was what she was. She was what was inside the circumference of the "O" of Olive. Why did they have to name her after something so small as an olive? It didn't matter. She'd forgiven her parents. She had done what they wanted her to do; she had gotten married. It was expected of her and she ought to do what was expected of her. She had tried to tell herself that she would be happy. But from the very beginning, her marriage hadn't given her what she expected. Had she really expected so much? She couldn't remember. She would go nuts if she kept trying to make sense out of it. She'd better push it out of her mind. She had to blank it out or she really would go nuts.

In private, Olive's parents talked about their daughter's strangeness. Then, Solomon Armsburg had spoken to Mortimer. Olive should have a baby. Her mother and he had given much thought to this. Mortimer agreed. He should have a son. A son that would be his partner someday.

In an effort to make Olive pregnant, Mortimer forced himself to have intercourse with her every night, and sometimes two or three times a night. Most of the time, Olive acted as though she'd been anesthetized.

At the end of a month, Olive menstruated. This troubled her. She wanted to become pregnant. She would be different; things would be better after she was pregnant.

In the succeeding months, when she did not become pregnant, Olive began to fear that she was failing as a woman. She didn't know what to do. Things were beyond her power. Something terrible would happen to her; she knew it. If only she could talk to someone. But she couldn't. She had to be silent. She dared not risk talking to anyone. By keeping silent, she knew she was giving them an excuse to say things about her. But by talking, she would give them a chance to say worse things. She was in a bad enough way as it was. Having a baby would save her. They would think she was all right if she could have a baby.

Olive had begun to think of "they" and "them." If "they" knew how crazy she was, "they" might send her away. Even if "they" didn't put her away, "they" would laugh at her and talk about her. Her terror grew. She dreaded going to bed at night. She dreaded what Mortimer would do to her. She wished she could get pregnant by doing it to herself. She had been able to give herself an orgasm. And she did this sometimes. But she felt ashamed afterwards. You weren't supposed to do it to yourself. She didn't understand why it was so wrong; she liked it. And she didn't like it when Mortimer was on top of her. Once when he had been on her, he'd acted like a wild man. He had punched her with his fist. She thought that he hated her but he had cried out with pleasure when he came. For a moment, she felt a thrill. His violence had aroused her. For the first time, she felt a stirring. But Mortimer's violence came to a quick end and he fell asleep. She lay there.

After four months of trying, Olive became pregnant.

Maybe she was just late. But she never had been before. Her periods had always been regular. She was pregnant. She just knew she was. Suppose something was wrong with her? What would happen to her baby?

—I'm not crazy.

But she was afraid that she might be. No, that wasn't it at all. She was afraid that "they" would think that she was and put her away. She had to stay on guard, not let them know anything about what she thought. She had to be very careful, not only for herself but for her baby.

Olive knew that both her father and mother wanted her to have a baby. They wanted a grandchild. People did when they started to get old. And maybe it was what she needed. No "maybe" about it; she did need a baby. Suddenly, the idea of having a child brought a gush of happiness. Hope flooded over her.

Olive surprised Mortimer. She talked more than she had in weeks. She asked him what he wanted to name the baby. She said she was sure it would be a boy. Mortimer said that they had plenty of time to decide and that they could wait. Olive said she had known she could have a baby. Mortimer said he had never said she couldn't. Olive didn't say anything to this. Then Mortimer went on to say that all he'd said was that they should wait until they had the baby before naming it. He was thinking of the kid. Once you gave a kid a name, that name stuck for life. Olive said she knew that. Mortimer asked her what it was that she knew. Olive said she knew that what he said was true. Mortimer didn't say anything. He didn't want to talk about naming the kid, not at this stage. Something could go wrong and he didn't want to spend time talking about something so far off.

FOUR

Olive Armsburg was living alone. She was lonely at times but she thought she would get used to it. She was going to be happy. Her son, Roy, was eight years old. He was away at the DeForest School for Boys in DeForest, Connecticut. She couldn't take care of him, not now. Her psychiatrist, Dr. Stein, had told her so. And Mortimer had wanted Roy away. He didn't want to keep Roy himself but he was against Roy's living with her. He only had one objection to Roy's going off to school, and Solomon Armsburg had removed that by agreeing to pay for his grandson's education. Mortimer Jameson claimed to love his son but he loved money more. That was one of the reasons why she divorced him. She should never have married him in the first place.

Mortimer had moved back to Pittsburgh. He had come and gone. And her mother had come and gone. She had died two years ago. Olive had been smashed up, bad for months. And then one morning she had awakened, and she hadn't felt all smashed up. Not long afterwards, she had been set back badly by her father. He'd married again. She didn't want a stepmother. But that was what she got. A stepmother fifteen years younger than her father.

Olive had not returned home to live after her divorce. Even if her father had not remarried, she wouldn't have gone back there. She wanted to be on her own. She never had been. On her own, she would be free. She had to feel free. She had to know that nobody was watching her.

And yet, Olive was hurt that she hadn't been asked to come back home. It didn't matter that she didn't want to go back. Neither her father nor Bernice knew this. They didn't care about her. She didn't care whether or not Bernice cared about her. But her father? That was different. He must never have cared about her. No wonder she had doubted herself sometimes. But she'd be all right now. She was going to have a better life. She was still a young woman; she was only thirty-three years old.

In her three-room apartment on East End Avenue on a sunny afternoon, Olive looked out the window. She saw the river sparkling with sunbeams on its surface.

Life begins at thirty-three, she told herself.

Olive began her days by getting up between seven and eight, taking a shower, attending to her toilet, and then cooking and eating her breakfast. The newspaper was delivered to her door and she usually read it as she ate.

Then, she would sit for a few minutes in a dreamy state.

Suddenly, when the impulse came, Olive would start to paint. Olive's painting was therapeutic, or at least gave signs of being therapeutic. Dr. Braverman, her new psychiatrist, said that it helped to strengthen her ego. Olive believed him.

Olive knew now that she had been sick, psychologically ill, and she was no longer ashamed. She believed she was getting well and that her painting was important.

Olive painted almost every day. Time went fast; sometime it was as if time did not exist. This in itself must be therapeutic, she thought, because time had often hung on her like the pendulum of a clock too heavy to swing. Time had always been like that. In her memory, Olive compressed time. She remembered it as slow and heavy because she'd had so little to do. She had been bored and restless. Time seemed to be forever. But that stage had passed. And the way that time flew when she was painting must be proof that she was getting well.

Olive's subject matter was a natural world of simple recognizable objects. She painted rooms with open windows and sunlight falling through the curtains. She did much of her painting in the morning because morning sunlight was pretty and bright. She painted flow-

ers—pansies, daisies, lilies, sweet peas, anemones, forget-me-nots.
There were tables and chairs. And often there was fruit, especially apples, because Cezanne had painted apples in his still lifes. Olive
was happy when she was painting. Sometimes she talked to herself
as she painted. There was nothing wrong with that. It didn't mean
anything. But who said that it did? Was there anything wrong with
her because she talked out loud? Nobody heard her, but suppose
someone did? Someone? Who was someone?

She was well; she was sound of mind. Dr. Braverman had all but
told her this. He had not seen her paintings but he had listened to
her describing them. Sometimes when she described something she
had painted or was going to paint, he would give a psychiatric
meaning, make a clinical interpretation, of what the subject matter meant.

Until about a year ago she hadn't been able to paint at all. And
even when she had started to paint again, she couldn't think of subjects. Dr. Braverman helped by suggesting subjects for her to paint.
And she had painted. She wanted to get well.

Olive no longer painted as though she were hanging on for dear
life. Her pictures were organized, constructed, arranged.

She was getting well; becoming an artist.

Becoming, hell, I am an artist, she thought one sunny noontime
as she was putting her brushes away.

In a sense, she was an artist. But what did that mean? Not much
unless she became a great artist. Being an artist didn't mean much
more, when all was said and done, than being a failure.

Olive shook her head. Such thoughts were bothersome; she
wouldn't waste her time thinking thoughts like these. She had come
a long way with her painting. She was almost well now, normal.

—What?

Olive turned. Had someone spoken? She thought she'd heard a
voice but she wasn't sure. She listened.

—Well, if you're going to say something, say it.

Nothing was said.

Olive's son, Roy, came to see her. He had spent the last few va-

cations with his father in Pittsburgh. Olive hadn't seen much of
him while she was so troubled herself. She didn't know how she
would react to seeing him. She hoped she would get to know him
again, and to love him. And that he would get to know her and
love her.

While Roy was visiting her, Phyllis Ryan telephoned to ask how
he was, and to ask if Olive would like to bring Roy over to see
Tommy. Olive agreed that this would be a good idea.

"Oh, Phyllis, it's wonderful having Roy home. He's really devoted
and he wants to do things for me."

"That's wonderful."

"He squeezed the oranges for my orange juice this morning and
even made the coffee," Olive said.

"Tommy would burn the house down if he tried to light the
stove."

"I think it's being in boarding school. When they come home,
they know they've missed you," Olive said.

"You might be right," Phyllis agreed. "When can you bring Roy
down to see Tommy?"

"I'll have to talk to Roy but he's not here," Olive said.

"What on heaven's name do you mean, Olive. You're Roy's mother; you can certainly make a date for him to come see his playmate."

"I know," Olive said.

She wanted to go. She would probably see Eddie; and she liked
Eddie Ryan.

"I'll call you back, Phyllis."

"I might not be home," Phyllis snapped.

Phyllis was irritated, Olive could tell. But she couldn't make the
decision. She just couldn't. If only . . .

"We'll make it tomorrow afternoon, Olive."

Phyllis' suggestion was more a command than a suggestion.

"Yes," Olive said.

"What time do you want to make it?"

"I don't know, Phyllis, what time do you want us?"

"Why don't you come at twelve? We'll have lunch and the two

boys can have lunch by themselves."
"All right, Phyllis, we'll try to make it."
"Oh for God's sake, Olive!"
Olive felt abashed.
"We'll be there, Phyllis."
"That's good; I'm sure the boys will enjoy it."

Roy Jameson was getting impatient. His mother was so slow and
pokey getting dressed. They were going down to see the Ryans.
He didn't particularly like Tommy Ryan but he was glad they were
going somewhere. He was a little bit bored with being with his
mother. Why couldn't she hurry? She was so slow about everything.
That's why he squeezed the oranges in the morning and made the
coffee. It took her so long to do anything. It was getting so he
couldn't stand it—her being so pokey.
Olive came out of the bedroom. She was ready. They left the
apartment, went downstairs, and got a taxicab to take them to the
Ryans on East Fifty-eighth Street.

"Hello, Tommy," Olive said matter-of-factly.
"Hello," Tommy Ryan answered.
Olive and Roy were standing outside the apartment door.
"Roy Jameson," Phyllis said with controlled enthusiasm.
"Hello," Roy said, thinking that Tommy's mother was funny,
too.
"Well come in, come in," Phyllis said, stepping aside to let them
pass.
Olive walked in, Roy followed her.
"Throw your things anywhere," Phyllis said, "it doesn't matter."
As she said this, Phyllis pointed to the bed in a small room off
the dining room. Olive took her hat and coat off and dropped them
on the bed. Roy and Tommy had gone to the front of the apart-
ment.

"Roy," Olive called.

Roy did not hear her.

"Roy," Olive called again.

"Yes, Mother."

"Bring your coat out here."

"It's all right, it's here."

"No, Roy, bring it back here," Olive called.

Roy brought his hat and jacket to the bedroom where his mother stood waiting for him.

"Put them on the bed with mine," Olive called.

Roy dropped them on the bed as he had been told and went back to the front of the apartment.

"And how are you, Olive?" Phyllis asked.

"Oh . . ."

She did not finish the sentence.

"I'll fix lunch now."

"I'm hungry," Olive told her.

"It will be ready quickly," Phyllis assured her.

"I haven't had any breakfast."

"Oh I'm sorry. I didn't know if you'd be on time or not and I didn't want to have everything done and not have you showing up until the food was cold."

"I'm always on time, Phyllis."

Olive's voice was very emphatic.

"Oh are you? I didn't know that."

"Yes I am. I'm always on time."

"Well, I didn't know. I'm sorry, Olive."

"That's all right."

Phyllis ran some water in a small pot, dropped several frankfurters into it, and put it on the gas range.

Lunch with Phyllis wasn't pleasant. Phyllis Ryan was too nervous, too something or other, for her. She gave Olive an uneasy feeling. She'd like to give it back to her but she was a little afraid of Phyllis.

But even though she wasn't comfortable with her, Olive stayed a long time. She kept hoping that Eddie Ryan would come home. Phyllis had said he'd gone out for a while and might be back. Besides, there was nothing else to do for the rest of the afternoon.

Tommy and Roy played for about an hour but then they lost interest in each other. Tommy went into his room and Roy stayed in the living room, looking out the window. Every so often, he'd call his mother and ask when they were going. She'd tell him they would be leaving soon. But after she told him this five or six times, she became angry when he called her.

"We'll go when I am ready. You'll wait," Olive called to him.

Phyllis asked Olive about her painting. Phyllis had seen some of her work once and had liked it. Olive told Phyllis that her painting was coming along fine and she invited Phyllis to come see her new work. Phyllis said that she would, just as soon as she was able. Olive said that she hoped it would be soon. Phyllis said that yes, it would be.

A few minutes after this conversation, Olive and Roy left. They walked to First Avenue to get a taxicab. Roy was sulking. He continued to sulk in the cab. Olive didn't notice this. She was thinking about Phyllis. If Phyllis didn't telephone soon, she would telephone and remind her. She would try to sell Phyllis one of her paintings when she came to look at them.

When the cab ride ended, Olive turned to her son: "Roy, I paid the fare down. Don't you think you should pay the fare back?"

"No, Mother, I don't."

"Well, I do," Olive said, opening the door.

She got out, leaving Roy to pay the fare.

Sulking, Roy Jameson paid for the ride.

FIVE

Shortly after Roy Jameson went back to school, Olive Armsburg went into a decline that suddenly turned into a tailspin. She was in a catatonic state. She was sent to a sanitarium in Connecticut where she was given electric shock treatments.

Even though there was no pain, Olive's fear of these treatments was intense. She would tremble when it was time to receive another one. Her terror was such that she couldn't speak. She would sit, rigid, afraid to move, in such dread that her mind was held fixed, like a stone. At other times she would crumple up on her bed and sob. As she sobbed, her body would shake in convulsive jerks. Fatigued from sobbing, she would give way to long, low moans. Sometimes she would moan herself to sleep.

But Olive began to remember. It was a painful process and it brought her torment. As she remembered, she was often disturbed. There were nights when she would try to tell herself things but then her voice would become other Voices and she could not make them stop. The Voices would not let her sleep. She would shriek at them, commanding them to shut up. At times she would plead with them, beg them to be quiet. Then, enraged, she would curse the Voices. This lasted for about six weeks.

Four months later Olive was released from the sanitarium.

Olive was afraid. She was afraid of what would happen to her. Where would she live? She didn't want to have to go home with her father. That wasn't true. She did want to go but she couldn't because of her stepmother. How could she live in the same house with her stepmother when her stepmother knew that she, Olive, was insane? And that's what her stepmother thought, Olive knew that. Don't ask her how she knew it. She knew it and that was all there was to it.

Where would she go?

As her father's automobile neared the city, Olive became nervous. Her father, watching her out of a corner of his eyes, caught this.

"Father?"

"Yes, Olive."

"I want to live in a hotel until I can get an apartment."

"Will you be all right in a hotel?"

"Yes, Father, I will be."

Her father thought for a moment.

"Please, Father."

Her voice sounded desperate. He wasn't sure what he should do. But he could see that she was disturbed about coming to his apartment.

"Oh my God, I almost forgot," her father exclaimed.

Olive looked at him.

"I promised Dr. Lustig that we would go by his office before we go any place," Mr. Armsburg said.

Olive smiled, sadly.

Olive's new psychiatrist was Dr. Henry Lustig. He was about forty years old but looked younger. He had a pleasant, open face. He wore expensive well-cut suits that were conservatively styled.

Dr. Lustig was waiting for Olive and her father. He had assured Mr. Armsburg earlier that had he been able to cancel some appointments, he would have gone with him to the sanitarium to pick up Olive.

When Olive entered his office, Dr. Lustig rose, and with a smile on his face, beckoned her to a chair on the other side of his desk. Mr. Armsburg had been asked to wait in the reception room.

Dr. Lustig sat down. He asked Olive how she was feeling. Olive didn't know; she was nervous and she guessed she was afraid.

What was she afraid of?

She didn't know. Couldn't you be afraid without being afraid of something? She was afraid to go home with her father, afraid to stay in his apartment with her stepmother. That was what she was afraid of, she guessed.

As she spoke to her doctor, Olive began to grow calm.

She told Dr. Lustig that she no longer felt afraid, but that she truly honestly felt that she would be less likely to become disturbed if she went to a hotel instead of going home with her father, to her stepmother.

Dr. Lustig watched Olive. He listened to her and asked her some questions. Then, he rang for his nurse. She appeared in an instant. He asked her to ask Mr. Armsburg if he would kindly step inside. The nurse went out. Soon, Mr. Armsburg entered Dr. Lustig's private office. Dr. Lustig asked him to have a seat, please.

"I am pleased about your daughter's condition, Mr. Armsburg," Dr. Lustig began.

Both Mr. Armsburg and Olive were surprised by this statement.

"That's good news Doctor. I'm glad to hear it," Mr. Armsburg said.

Olive said nothing but she smiled. She trusted Dr. Lustig; he wouldn't let anything bad be done to her. She felt safe, almost safe, here in his office.

"Where would you like to go, Olive? Where would you like to stay?" Dr. Lustig asked.

Olive was silent. Where did she want to stay? They were waiting for her answer.

She wanted to tell them what she had already told them; she wanted to tell them that she did not want to go to her father's apartment, to where her stepmother lived. But they were both watching her. Her father was watching her. This made her nervous.

"As your daughter's doctor, I think that I should help her make up her mind," Dr. Lustig said, turning to Olive's father.

Olive's face brightened.

"You are the doctor, of course, that's what we're paying you for," Mr. Armsburg said.

Olive frowned. She didn't like the reference to money.

Dr. Lustig spoke: "I would advise that Olive, until she can get her bearings, stay at a good hotel in this area. She can find an apartment that she likes and fix it up to her satisfaction.

Mr. Armsburg nodded.

"Whatever you say, Doctor. Your word is final."

SIX

Olive was happy. She liked living at the Hotel Wharton. It was not a big hotel but her suite was large and comfortable. The service was good. But then it should be; she was paying thirty-five dollars a day.

She was free. If she wanted to go for a walk, she could. If she wanted to stroll down the streets of New York, there was nothing to stop her. Not that she would, not yet. She was afraid to go out on the street. She had promised Dr. Lustig that before she did go out, she would telephone him first. She was going to keep her promise. She was scared not to. She didn't want to be sent back to the sanitarium. She wanted no more of that. She was not going to take any chances. Besides, she didn't want to go out. Not yet. Eventually she would go for a walk, see people and look at the store windows. But not for a while yet. Someone might see her and not like her. They might laugh at her, even hurt her. She might say something wrong or do something wrong. She didn't know what, but something. She couldn't be sure of people. They were strange, too.

Olive went to the window. It had turned gray outside. Her rooms were high.

—High enough.

She lit a cigarette. What had she been thinking about? Oh yes, people, what they were like.

Suddenly, Olive felt weird. It was as if she wasn't there. Should it be weren't here? Which was correct? She used to know. What was wrong with her? Why did she feel this way? Why had she let the strangeness from the outside get into her head? She would have to be more careful because, oh God, she didn't want to go back to the sanitarium.

She wasn't going to wilt like a lily in a hotel room. She'd go out. She was free now, and living in a hotel, not a sanitarium. Sanitarium! It was no better than a pig's sty. A real loony bin! And she wasn't loony.

Prove it, a voice inside her said.

"Goddamn it, I will," she answered.

Olive had been sitting on the sofa smoking. She jumped up and walked toward the closet for her hat and coat. Suddenly she stopped. She should dress up for this special occasion. She should knock them dead when she made her first appearance. But she didn't have much with her.

Olive put on extra makeup. She smeared on lipstick heavily. Then she put on her hat and coat and went downstairs.

She was knocking them dead. She could tell from the way people turned to stare at her. She smiled. She took a few steps from the hotel entrance. A lot of people were on the sidewalk. Some of them looked at her. The men. She took a few more steps, walking slowly. She didn't want them to think she was running away from them. Goddamn it, she'd show them, she'd walk very slowly.

Olive walked on. There was a man behind her. She could feel his eyes on her back. He was following her. Well why shouldn't he? He didn't think she was crazy. She didn't dare turn around. No telling what might happen.

Olive turned and smiled. He was wearing a gray coat and he was following her, all right. She turned at the next corner. She was dying to look back again but she didn't. He was still following her. Why in hell shouldn't he? She was a woman, wasn't she?

Olive turned around. He was nowhere in sight. The man in the gray coat was nowhere in sight. He must have given up because he couldn't get her to go with him. Olive stood in the center of the sidewalk, staring vacantly. Suddenly, she felt frightened. She hurried back to the hotel.

People doing simple things looked odd to Olive. They talked, laughed, crossed streets, got in and out of elevators, sat down, ate, shopped in stores, rode in automobiles. She saw people dodging traffic, crossing streets, waiting for red lights to turn green. She had done these things and would be able to do them again. She knew that. Dr. Lustig told her that she could. And he told her that she must take things, one by one, a little at a time.

Dr. Lustig brought up the question of her finding an apartment. Olive was surprised. She liked living in the Wharton. She wasn't sure she could manage an apartment yet. She looked at him questioningly.

"I'm afraid, Dr. Lustig."

"Afraid, Olive? Or suspicious?"

Olive's face went blank.

"It's suspicion, too, isn't it, Olive?"

She grinned. Her grin was an admission.

"Our time is up, Olive," Dr. Lustig said, his voice changing to a casual and businesslike tone.

Olive's face fell.

"Our next step, then, is your apartment."

"Yes," Olive said, meekly.

Olive found an apartment on West Seventy-ninth Street, a half block from Central Park West. It was on the tenth floor of a large, old, but well-kept building. There was no doorman but there were elevator operators. Olive's apartment had four rooms, two of them large, with a good-sized kitchen and bathroom. The rent was one hundred and sixty-five dollars a month.

Once she found her own apartment, Olive began to feel better. She looked forward to living in it, and to painting again. It was a challenge.

Olive desperately wanted to get well. If she didn't she'd be sent back. She couldn't face that again. Oh God. No, she'd never forget those shock treatments. She still woke up at night sweating all over.

Getting set in her new apartment kept Olive busy. She had little time to think of the sanitarium or of shock treatments. She had to be *there* to receive deliveries. She had to arrange things in her apartment.

In a couple of weeks, the new apartment was settled.

I'm all set to go now, she told herself.

Olive resumed her painting. Her work changed; it no longer followed the same course. It was surrealistic now. She used somber colors and the shapes were weird. Sometimes they looked like swollen organs. Many were distorted but barely concealed genitalia.

She no longer felt the same lightness she remembered feeling when she had first started to paint. She could remember when it made her happy to paint but she was thinking back before her terrible days of horror. She could still remember the horror. Those had been awful days, she wouldn't think of them. She would remember the light happy feeling she'd had when she had started. She wished she still got that feeling. Now when she worked, she felt a great strain. But the painting she was doing now was more important. This was why she was so tense. This was why there was so much gloom and sadness on her canvas. There was gloom and sadness in life.

Dr. Lustig had given her some green and white capsules. She took one in the morning and another one when she was tired or depressed. Dr. Lustig had told her that she could take a third one if she needed it but that she should not take more than three a day. She could get a counter effect if she did. Instead of pepping her up, that fourth pill could work the other way. She wasn't going to take any chances. She could always have a drink or two. A few drinks bucked her up and helped her get over the blues.

There were a number of bars in the neighborhood. At first, Olive was too timid to go in. She thought of going into Hennessey's, around the corner on Amsterdam Avenue. A few times, she walked by the place, looked in the window, and started toward the door. But then she would walk on.

One day, Olive walked in. Four men were drinking at the bar. Olive ordered a beer. The bartender, a dark-haired man with an Irish face, served her. The men stopped talking when Olive walked in. They avoided looking at her but she stared and smiled at them, one by one. No one spoke. She drank her beer, paid for it, and left, calling back a "thank you."

Who were those men to treat her like that? Ignorant Irishmen. In case anyone wanted to know, she happened to be the daughter of a millionaire. And a damned good woman, too.

She didn't want to go back to her apartment on the tenth floor.

—Tenth floor.

The number troubled her. There was something about it she didn't like. It was jinxed.

She walked toward Central Park West. But by the time she reached it, she decided it was too cold to walk in the Park. It was too cold to walk period. She returned to her apartment.

—Hennessey's is not the only bar on Manhattan Island.

Olive had been sitting in her living room for a few minutes. She laughed. As if she had to tell herself there was another bar in town. She would go out again but this time, she'd dress up.

Olive walked into O'Malley's. There were more people here and they were a better class. She could tell. And she liked the little bartender's smile. His name was Joe.

There was a blonde at the opposite end of the bar. She was good looking but when she smiled, you could see that she needed a dentist. A well-dressed man at her side was trying to get some place with her. But the blonde wasn't interested.

Olive finished her drink and pushed her glass forward. She tried to get the bartender's eye but he was talking to the man making the play for the blonde.

"Joe," the man at Olive's left called out.

Joe turned.

"The lady wants a drink," the man said.

"Oh!" Joe exclaimed. Turning to Olive. "Yes, Madame?"

"Another martini, please."

"Yes, ma'am," Joe said, taking her glass.

Olive smiled. She turned to the man and thanked him. He told her that she was welcome.

Joe served Olive her drink. She took a sip, leaned back, and reached into her pocketbook for a cigarette. She was searching for a match when the man next to her held up a lighter.

"May I?"

Olive thanked him.

He was trying to make her; she could tell. Well, she'd talk to him and be pleasant enough but if he thought he was going to lay her, he had another thought coming.

She took another sip of her drink.

"Nasty weather, isn't it?" the man remarked.

"Yes, it is a nasty day."

She took another sip. She liked the way it spread a warm feeling into her stomach. It felt good. She smiled. The man moved a little closer. She noticed, but she didn't mind. She was glad that he was interested.

He finished his drink and ordered another one.

"It's a mean day, all right," he said.

Joe served him a fresh martini.

The blonde at the other end of the bar stood. Olive watched her. The man next to her seemed to have given up. That's what it looked like to her, Olive thought. But wait a minute, he's getting up too.

They walked out together.

The man beside Olive noticed the other two leaving together. He looked at Olive. She returned the look. He raised his eyebrows. Olive smiled and drained her glass.

"Are you leaving us?" he asked her.

"My apartment is cozy," Olive said.

The bartender appeared with a check in his hand.

"I'll take it, Joe," the man said, taking a five-dollar bill from his wallet.

Olive put on her coat.

"Want company?" he asked.

"Aren't you going to be my company?"

Olive's smile was almost grotesque.

SEVEN

H is name was Jacob Schaeffer.

Inside her apartment, Olive took his hat and coat and hung them up. Jacob Schaeffer looked around the large living room. He was surprised. She was no ordinary pickup, that was for sure. There was something odd about her. The weird paintings on the wall. And that smile. Maybe he shouldn't stay. She wasn't a whore; she was a painter. Still, if she wanted to be fucked . . . he had picked her up for that. But those paintings on the wall.

To hell with them, he'd stay.

Jacob Schaeffer sat down and waited for Olive to bring him a drink. She was in the kitchen. He could hear her opening and closing the refrigerator. In a moment she appeared with martinis on a tray.

"Thank you," he said, taking one.

Olive took the other one and sat down on the couch, facing him across a low glass-topped table.

"Well," Olive said, lifting her glass, "here's to something or other."

Jacob Schaeffer raised his glass.

It was good, a good martini.

"How is your drink, Mr. Schaeffer?"

"Good. You make a good martini."

"I know I do."

He took another sip and looked at her. He'd better say something, sitting here like this wasn't going to make her want to climb into bed with him.

"Are you a painter?"

"I should think so," Olive answered.

"I thought so when I saw these paintings."

"Do you like painting?" Olive asked.

"I don't know anything about the subject, I'm sorry to say."

"I didn't think so," Olive took another sip.

"What makes you say that?"

He had half a mind to clear out. But he didn't. For a fuck, I don't have to be crazy about her, he thought.

"I didn't mean to be rude, Mr. Schaeffer."

"That's all right."

He lifted his martini. Olive took a big swallow of hers. Jacob Schaeffer noticed. There was no point in leaving now.

Olive finished her drink.

"Drink up, Jacob, let's have another one."

He hesitated.

"I thought you liked my martinis."

"I do."

"So drink up." Olive's voice was aggressive.

Maybe he ought to leave. Something about her. He finished his drink and handed her the glass. She poured two more martinis. Handing his back, she bent forward and brushed a kiss across his forehead. She returned to the couch, sat, and picked up her own drink.

Suppose she was just a tease? The little bitch, why, he'd . . .

"What are you thinking, Mr. Schaeffer?"

"What are *you* thinking?"

"The same thing you're thinking," Olive smiled.

"Maybe," he said.

"If you sit closer, I won't have to talk so loud," Olive said.

He laughed and went to sit beside her. He put his glass down on the table.

"Lift your glass," Olive said.

Oh God, it's been so long, she thought.

He put his hand on her thigh and leaned toward her.

"Let's go into the bedroom," Olive whispered.

He was gone. She felt good. She felt guilty too but she felt really good. She had been hungry for a man. And she had had one. She would have more, too. Whenever she wanted one. She could look forward to it. She smiled.

Suddenly, Olive frowned. What was the something she could look forward to? She couldn't remember. She looked perplexed. Then she laughed.

"Oh yes, I remember," she said aloud, "I'm looking forward to getting laid any damned time I feel like getting laid."

On that, she would have another drink. Going to the kitchen, Olive laughed again.

Olive went to bed around nine-thirty. She felt good. And she woke up feeling good. Life had become a little more interesting. She had something to look forward to. Any time she wanted to, she could go pick up another man at a bar. And she would.

Olive hummed as she squeezed orange juice.

Later, as she read the paper, she smiled. Sex had done her a world of good. She had an appointment with Dr. Lustig this morning. What would he say when she told him?

Olive entered Dr. Lustig's office smiling. He told her that she looked happy this morning. She said that she was happy; she told him about Jacob Schaeffer.

"Are you in love with Jacob Schaeffer?"

"God no. I picked him up because I wanted to be fucked."

"And?"

"And I got a good fucking."

Olive watched Dr. Lustig's face. Was he shocked? No he wasn't. She was disappointed. But she would have been more disappointed if he had been, she guessed.

Dr. Lustig did not tell her that her sexual experience was good for her. There was much more that she needed than sex. However, Jacob Schaeffer had offered her something; he had bolstered her morale.

Olive was still happy when she left Dr. Lustig's office. She walked along Park Avenue for a block or two. She thought of home, her father's home. It had been her home but it wasn't any more. The smile vanished. Suddenly she was afraid. She stepped over to the curb, waving frantically for a cab. Several passed but they all held passengers. Her voice grew shrill as she called:

"Taxi! Taxi!"

Finally one stopped. Olive got in and sank back in the seat. She was going to her own apartment. Her fear was gone. Olive gave the address to the driver.

She was always depressed after a visit to Dr. Lustig, but not this depressed. Why had she been so afraid on Park Avenue? She had felt menaced. She didn't feel that way now but she was exhausted. She didn't have the energy to get up and do anything. She sat, wishing she could snap out of it. She was so tired. Why? It was getting dark outside. It would be pitch black in a little while. She ought to turn on the lights. All she had to do was get up, walk about two feet, maybe three, and turn on the lights. Or she could walk over to the end table and turn on the lamp. She really should force herself to do it.

Slowly, Olive rose to her feet. She walked to the bathroom and turned on the light. In the mirror, she saw a strange face, a face that looked like her but wasn't. She opened the medicine cabinet and took out the bottle with the green and white capsules. She filled a glass of water and then set it down on the sink. She took a dexamyl capsule out of the bottle, put it in her mouth and washed it down.

Which was worse? To be listless and sad or to be all pepped up with nothing to do and no place to go. She didn't know. The dexamyl had pepped her up and now she was restless. She could go to a bar. But no, she didn't want to do that. She had to do something. Olive launched into a fury of housecleaning.

EIGHT

It was more than a week since she had picked up Jake Schaeffer. He had made her feel good. She hadn't been bothered by sex for a whole week. Funny, maybe she should say curious, but she didn't want to go out and find him again. She didn't feel like it.

—But you will, ol' gal, you will.

Olive painted every day even though it depressed her. She was making progress; she was certain of that, but she didn't like to paint in her apartment.

Olive decided to find a studio.

She had worked enough. She needed a man again. It was a sunny afternoon.

Olive fortified herself with two drinks before she left the apartment. She decided not to return to O'Malley's; she didn't want to be taken for a whore. She wasn't. A whore charged money. She'd have to get to know several bars, but that should be easy enough to do. She should be positive, think with confidence. It would help her to get well. She was getting better, she knew that.

On the street, Olive's confidence wavered. She walked about four blocks, and then hailed a cab.

"Where to, lady?"

—Where?

"Eighth Street," she told him.

It was the first thing that came to mind.

"Eighth and where?"

"Eighth Street and Sixth Avenue."

The cab driver drove her there. When she paid him, he gave

her two quarters in change. She handed him one and asked:

"May I have change for this, please?"

Annoyed, the driver gave her change.

"Here," Olive said, handing him a dime.

He took it without speaking. Olive got out of the cab.

She found herself in front of a drug store. Now where? Where would she go? The street was crowded but there always were a lot of people on Eighth Street. There were enough men for her to find one. But she couldn't just stand on a street corner and expect some man walking along the street to go mad over her. The thing to do was to find the right kind of bar.

The right kind of bar, Olive thought ironically.

That was a laugh. She should have taken a second look at the name of the place before she had walked in. She turned toward the window.

CONTRARY MARY'S, she read.

She drank her martini and looked around. There were about eight other customers in the bar, all of them fairies. They weren't saying much. They had clammed up when she had walked in. She'd clam up too if she were a goddamned fairy. She couldn't stand fags. She'd like to get out of this place but she wasn't going to leave her martini. She didn't care if these little faggots liked it or not. Her martini wasn't bad. Even a faggot bartender ought to be able to make a decent martini. What else could he do for a woman? She didn't like the way those two pansies were looking at her. She'd finish her drink and get hell out of Contrary Mary's.

How disgusting! A fat middle-aged fag making eyes at a boy who couldn't be over twenty-one. And the boy was flirting back.

At the opposite end of the bar, two other fags were talking.

"But my dear, on my honor ..."

That was it! She had had enough. Olive finished her drink, paid for it, and left. About halfway between Sixth and Fifth Avenues, Olive saw a big bar named Main Street. She walked in. Most of the customers were men.

Everything in pants isn't a man, she reminded herself.

It was so noisy she couldn't hear herself think. But she liked it. It was exciting. Things were happening.

—Or going to happen.

There had been such a crowd around the bar that Olive couldn't get served. A fellow had gotten her a martini and when she had tried to pay for it, told her to forget it. He was nice enough looking but he'd gotten lost in the shuffle.

Three other men were yakking in her ears. Well, they could keep right on yakking.

"Are there any more at home like you?" asked one of them. He was middle-aged.

"No, I have no sister," Olive answered.

"They made you and threw away the mold, did they?"

"That's right," she smiled.

"So the world will have to do with just one of you," another man said.

Olive turned to look at him.

"What's your name, babe?" the first man asked.

"Olive."

"Ripe Olive," he laughed.

"How do you know I'm ripe?" Olive asked.

His friend, who was younger, about thirty, and good looking, gave her a look.

"By the evidence of my eyes," the first man said.

Olive lifted her glass and tried not to show that his remark hurt.

"Maybe you need glasses," she quipped.

Some men nearby laughed.

Olive held up her empty glass.

"Here, Olive, let me get you another drink. What is it you're drinking?"

"Martini."

He ordered for her.

Olive thanked him when he handed her her drink. A few drops spilled on her hand. She took a stiff gulp.

After she had finished her drink, Olive said she was going home.

"Why don't you stay?"

It was too noisy for her, too crowded. She smiled at the two men standing near her.

They followed her outside. Olive walked slowly. They caught up with her. She pretended to be surprised.

"If you don't have anything else to do or any place to go, come to my place. I can fix martinis."

They accepted her invitation and introduced themselves—Bentley Catman and Jesse Elmstein.

She shouldn't have brought these two strange men home. It wasn't smart, not smart at all. They looked respectable enough, but still. Oh, they wouldn't hurt her. But that wasn't what she was afraid of. One of them could steal something while she was in bed with the other one. What should she do? She didn't know what worried her more, the fact that she had brought home two men to fornicate the same night or the fact that one of them might steal something. Well, she had brought them home to lay and she might as well go through with it.

"Let's have some fun, Olive," Bentley said.

"What do you mean by fun?"

"Bedroom fun," he answered.

"Oh that," Olive laughed.

"Don't you like to have fun?"

"Possibly."

"Don't count me out," Jesse chimed in.

"I'll sit next to you on the couch," Bentley said, standing.

"What about your friend?" Olive asked.

"Oh I'll sit on the other side," Jesse said.

They moved over to the couch. As Bentley reached over to kiss her, Jesse's hand moved under her dress.

On Sunday night, Olive dined with her father and stepmother. This was always a strain for her. Olive didn't realize that it was a strain for them as well.

Eventually, Sunday nights became more bearable. Olive grew somewhat used to them. And her father and Bernice became more accustomed to these Sunday night dinners. But there was still an undercurrent of tension. All three of them were careful about what they said.

Dinner had gone off well on this Sunday night. Solomon Armsburg believed that his daughter was getting better. He didn't know how much better; he was no doctor but he felt that there was some improvement. He certainly hoped so. Some people thought that his second marriage had something to do with Olive's breakdown. He was afriad that Olive herself thought this; she had been very upset when he had married Bernice.

Olive was a disappointment. She always had been. But didn't her breakdown explain this disappointment? It should. He didn't know what the full explanation was. He wasn't sure that these expensive doctors did either. Poor Olive. He didn't like to think about her, about what she had become.

Bernice Armsburg did not like Olive. Olive disliked her from the very beginning and Bernice responded in kind.

Bernice, a simple and friendly woman, was plain looking and plump. Her first husband, a jewelry salesman named Mike Ash, was killed in an automobile accident. They had no children. Mike Ash left her with a small but adequate income. She lived alone for years and had been lonely. There was no one to do things for, to talk to. It was no way for a woman to live.

After Hannah died, Solomon Armsburg thought that he was the loneliest man in the world. He was rich and he was free; but he sat in his big apartment, alone, night after night. He would read for a while and then go to the window and stare. He would go to the theater and come home to an empty apartment. Go out to dinner and come home to the same empty apartment.

Then, at a dinner party, he met Bernice Ash.

Lonely people, Bernice Ash would reflect later, must have a way of recognizing each other. She and Solomon Armsburg were drawn to one another from the very beginning. They talked. He asked her if she would dine with him. She accepted. He took her to dinner at Chambord's. That was the beginning. They began to dine together often. And they spoke on the telephone almost daily. It was not so much a courtship as it was a mutual recognition.

Bernice had heard about Olive the very first time she had dined with Solomon. He hadn't told her much but he had mentioned his daughter. It was evident to Bernice from the way he spoke that he was concerned and baffled by Olive. Bernice knew that she would have trouble with the girl. At first, this had worried her. She had not yet met Olive.

It was not so much what Solomon said about the girl; it was what he didn't say. Bernice hoped that her first unfavorable impression of Olive would turn out to be wrong when she met her. She would like to help the girl. Olive was evidently in some kind of trouble. Solomon was worried about her; Bernice could see that. Well, she certainly intended to try to help his daughter if she could.

Solomon Armsburg arranged for them to meet. He invited them both to dinner. He asked Florabelle, the *schvartze*, to cook a special meal.

It was a rainy Sunday evening. Bernice had taken a cab to Solomon's apartment. She had many doubts and uncertainties. When the taxi stopped in front of the building in which Solomon Armsburg lived, she stepped out with some trepidation.

Now. Now she would meet Olive.

Bernice Ash expected Olive to be much prettier. And Olive expected Bernice to be better looking. The two women were both relieved and disappointed in each other's looks.

Bernice Ash had been in the apartment only a few minutes when she knew that Olive could not disrupt her relationship with Solomon. During these same minutes, Olive came to fear Bernice. She understood, as Bernice had, that she could do nothing about this woman. And Bernice could do something about her.

The dinner went off without any unpleasantness, but there was a strain. Olive spoke only when spoken to. Solomon could think of very little to say. Bernice tried to guide the conversation.

It was apparent to both Solomon Armsburg and Olive what Bernice was doing but neither of them objected. Bernice was trying to help them. She was trying to keep a conversation going. Olive saw clearly that this woman had gotten her father. She was on her own now. But then hadn't she been before? Olive wished she could leave; she wanted to be by herself. But she would have to stay for a little while longer.

First there were cocktails. For dinner, they had roast beef, boiled potatoes, asparagus, and a salad. The meal was good; they should have enjoyed it, but they didn't because of Olive. Florabelle didn't like Olive. Olive had never paid much attention to her.

Florabelle had made something of a fuss over Olive when she had come in but she hadn't been able to keep up the pretense in the face of Olive's disinterest. She had stopped abruptly, gone back into the kitchen, saying that she hoped they would all like the dinner she had prepared for them.

Olive jabbed at her food. She was too upset to eat. Her father and his lady friend didn't seem to mind. She wished she could eat like they did.

Her father mentioned that Olive was a painter.

"Oh, that's interesting," Bernice said.

Olive didn't like this. He must have told her this before. Why did Bernice act surprised? Sounded like something prearranged. Her father didn't want her to know that he and his lady friend had talked about her. What else did this woman know about her?

"Do you have any of her paintings here?" Bernice asked.

Olive was embarrassed. She hoped her father was. He admitted he had none of Olive's paintings. Olive grew sad. He had never thought to ask her for one and she could not suggest it. The woman would know now just how little there was between her father and her. That might be why she'd asked the question. It made Olive mad. But getting mad wouldn't do her any good, no good at all.

She had to be very, very careful. Her anger could be turned against
her. They could say she'd had a relapse and that they would have
to put her away again. Olive turned toward Bernice Ash and smiled
emptily.

My God, thought Bernice. That smile!

Solomon Armsburg was talking about hanging one of Olive's
paintings. He said he'd like to hang one or two of them. Olive smiled
again, blankly. She had no intentions of letting him hang one of
her pictures, not now. But she didn't want him to know how she
felt. She had to keep smiling.

They finished their coffee.

Solomon suggested a brandy. Bernice said that she would like
one, and Olive decided to have one, too. Her father was living it up,
Olive thought. When her mother was alive, her father and mother
didn't drink brandy after dinner.

"This is good brandy," Olive said.

"Yes, it's one of my favorites, Courvoisier."

My God, at this age, her father was becoming a *bon vivant*. She
mustn't get mad, though. They'd say she was crazy. She'd concentrate on her drink.

Olive's lips trembled.

Had they noticed? Had the woman seen it? Olive took another
sip. She was frightened. If she didn't get out of here, she would
make a slip. She would say something.

The brandy slid down, warm. It made her feel a little better.
She'd have another glass.

Olive poured herself another brandy.

Olive didn't like to think about her father and Bernice Ash. It
made her too mad. And it made her sad, too. She remembered that
first dinner she had with them. She felt so lonely that night. She
hadn't enjoyed the dinner at all. But now she didn't mind the Sunday night dinners so much. Rain or shine, every Sunday night at
seven, she went to dinner there. The dutiful daughter. Who was
doing the fooling? Who was being fooled? They both seemed to
like it a lot. Well she didn't. She ought to know by now that her

feelings were the last thing to be taken into consideration.

To make it worse, her father started having other people in on Sunday evenings. At first, Olive felt it was done deliberately to humiliate her. But soon, she got over this. Most of the time now, Sunday night dinners did not bother her too much.

She had reached a decision. She didn't care. She might as well have her fling. And even if her fling amounted to no more than sex and booze, what of it? She liked it. She needed this kind of fling once in a while. It made her feel free. She had to be free, to escape. She didn't know how all this would end but she wasn't clear about a lot of things. She didn't know what to think. It was like not knowing where she was. In a sense, she didn't know where she was. It was confusing. She was mixed up, but everybody got mixed up at one time or another. Being mixed up was not the same as being crazy. She wasn't crazy. And she wasn't psychotic. Psychotic was just a polite word for crazy.

NINE

From time to time, Olive thought of Eddie Ryan. She liked to show him her paintings; she liked to hear him talk. Sometimes, she would lose what he said and stop listening. Often, she didn't listen to people. No matter what they were talking about, her thoughts would wander. But this wasn't what had caused her breakdown—or whatever it was called. It couldn't have been. As far back as she could remember, she had never been a good listener, even when she was a little girl. She just wasn't a listener. Most people weren't, so she was like other people. This was a kind of a feather in her cap, she'd say. She was like other people. Other people were like her. Maybe everybody was crazy.

Olive would always laugh aloud when she thought this. It was a very funny, very private joke. Of course her joke could be true, more true than she or anyone else would care to admit. But a joke, true or not, was not worth worrying about. Not worth caring about, either. There was no use in caring, no use at all.

And if she wasn't going to worry or care, she could be cheerful. She could be goddamned cheerful. And why be cheerful alone? She'd fix herself up and go have a drink at some bar. Then, she would cheerfully wait and see what happened after that.

Olive held her drink. She was in a bar on Lexington Avenue near Fifty-eighth Street.

The bartender was a thin, bald man with glasses. He had handed her her second martini with obvious disapproval.

Who was he to disapprove of her? He was only a bartender. She should be upset by what a bartender thought of her, Olive Armsburg.

Phew to you, she thought as she raised her glass. Phooey.

She glanced up and down the bar to see if there were any worth-while men. It didn't look too promising. She'd like something better than the poor pickings here. Maybe she ought to try another bar. She would after she finished this drink. What if the pickings were no better in another bar? It would be pretty depressing to go to a second bar and find the pickings as bad, or even worse.

Olive finished her martini.

She ordered a third one. She would stay where she was and take her chances.

She looked around again. There were about ten men at the bar. She was the only woman. For all she knew, they might think the pickings were poor, too. Let them.

The bartender served her another drink. Olive took a swig. She felt it going down. At least the martinis were good.

She picked up her pack of Marlboros. As she took out a ciga-rette, a man on her left moved closer to her.

"May I?" he asked, holding a match in front of her.

"Why not?"

She wouldn't go home alone tonight.

"Thank you," she said.

"My pleasure."

They exchanged smiles. That settled it. She would not be going back to the tenth-floor apartment alone.

He asked Olive her name. She told him. He told her to call him Merton Nydol. Olive said that she would, she would call him Mer-ton Nydol. He said that he would call her Olive. In that case, Olive told him, she would call him Merton.

"Where do you live, Olive?"

"On Seventy-ninth Street, Merton."

"Alone?"

"Yes, alone."

"And what do you do, Olive?"

"I paint."

Olive lifted her drink and took another swallow.

"Well I'll say one thing," Merton said, "you drink like a man."

"Or maybe men drink like women." Olive suggested.

"I don't connect."

"I mean that it could be that men drink like women instead of women drinking like men," Olive explained.

"I still don't get it."

"Skip it."

"Wait a minute, now I think I connect," Merton said.

"Do you?"

"I think so."

Olive didn't know what to say. She finished her drink.

"May I order you another one?" he asked.

"I believe I've had enough."

Seeing the look on his face, Olive was tempted to have one more, but she was afraid to.

"You won't change your mind?" he persisted.

"Oh all right, one more."

Merton Nydol signaled the bartender.

She wished she had never seen him. He was gone now but the memory of him made her shudder. He was one of those, a back door, kitchen boy. It had been horrible. Olive began to sob.

—Ohhh, how awful it had been!

Olive was sober. The shock and the pain had sobered her. She walked into the living room and poured a brandy to bolster herself. She was not so shaky now, but she had really been shaky before. If only she hadn't had so much to drink. Those last two martinis had been her downfall. What would Dr. Lustig say when she told him? She didn't know if she'd have the guts. But she had felt this way before. Something would happen or she'd do something and she'd be afraid to tell him, or so she'd think. Then, when she was in his office, she'd blurt it right out.

She was better now, much better. She didn't have the shakes any more. She'd gotten over them. That must mean something—it

must mean that she could take whatever she had to take.
Olive poured herself another brandy. She had survived what had
threatened to shatter her. That should prove something, shouldn't
it?
Suppose it did? What good did it do for her to sit and think of
all this damned rot?

Olive fell asleep after drinking almost half a bottle of brandy.
She slept long and deeply. She dreamed strange dreams but when
she awakened, she could not remember any more than that her
dreams had been strange.
The sun was shining on a new day. She didn't want to get up;
she felt like going back to sleep but she knew she couldn't. She lay
in bed until finally, she had to get up and go to the bathroom.
Olive came out of the bathroom feeling very much awake. She
felt better now. She was surprised. She went into the kitchen and
fixed herself a big breakfast. She ate heartily. Then she washed the
dishes.
Once dressed, she sat down and began sketching for a painting.
An idea had come to her. She wouldn't have believed she could work
this morning. Maybe Dr. Lustig could explain it to her—why she
could work after a night like last night. She had gotten a lot of
things out of her system. That cleaned the deck for work.
Olive sketched for over two hours. The sketches were intricately
involved and full of shapes. Some of them looked like internal organs placed in odd positions.
When she began to tire, she stopped. She looked at what she had
done. She had accomplished something. It made her feel good.
Olive went for a long walk in Central Park.

Olive had rented a studio over a store across town, on Lexington
Avenue in the Seventies. She took her sketches there and began to
work on a new painting. The work went well.

As Olive worked, her thoughts became less erratic. She was not as depressed as she had been. She felt the way other people did. Wait a minute, didn't she always think like other people? She wasn't so sure of this always but she was now. She didn't mind admitting that there were times when she wasn't like other people and that there was something wrong with her. But she didn't feel like that now. She must be all right. Oh she hoped so. She would be so happy. And it wasn't merely a question of her being happy, it was a matter of her life.

Olive was painting a large canvas. It was the painting for which she had made her first sketches the morning after bringing that Merton Nydol home. This picture was going to be important. It was already important to her.

Day after day, Olive worked on it. She did not yet have a title.

By Tuesday of the second week, the picture began to take on shape and form. It was turning out to be morbid. There were suggestions of decay in patches of brown and purple but Olive was not aware of this. There were times, however, when she became morbid as she worked on it. She did not associate these feelings with the picture. To Olive, the picture was sad. But it was incomplete.

The painting became a burden to her. She began to resist going to the studio. And once there, she could work for just a little while.

On some days, however, Olive would wake up eager to paint. She would fix her breakfast, eat, get dressed, and leave her apartment. If the weather was good, she would walk over to her studio on Lexington Avenue. Otherwise, she'd catch the crosstown bus. Or a taxi. As soon as she was in her studio, she would start work immediately.

Olive still had not given a title to this picture.

One rainy morning, Olive hurried to her studio in a taxi. She stared at her painting. She knew that it was completed. She would call it *Purple and Brown*.

Olive was happy. She had just finished her most important work.

It was an accomplishment. An achievement. *Purple and Brown* was a work of art. She had become an artist. If she hadn't been an artist before, she couldn't have painted it. She knew this. What she meant was that she had become an artist in a special sense. With this picture, she'd begun to realize her own style. She had begun to probe her own depths. She was on the edge of something important. She had never felt like this before.

Olive was tired. She had walked back from the studio. When she had reached her apartment, she had gone into the bedroom and changed clothes. She would take it easy.

She picked up a book that was lying on a table in the living room. It was a rental library book. Every day she kept it added to its cost. She didn't much like it but she had started it, and she was going to have to pay for it anyway, so she might as well finish it.

Olive started to read. What an awful book. And it got worse as it went on instead of better. But she was going to finish it. It was a challenge. And it would be wasteful and uneconomical not to finish it.

She read on for a couple of hours. She grew sleepy but she managed to stay awake long enough to finish it.

It stinks, Olive thought, but she had proven something.

She would take the book back first thing tomorrow.

Olive leaned back in the chair and closed her eyes.

"*Purple and Brown,*" she said aloud.

—It ought to be *Purples and Browns*; it was more than one purple, more than one brown.

"It's *Purple and Brown,*" she told herself, "not *Purples and Browns.*"

—It should be *Purples and Browns.*

"Who painted the picture, you or me? If I say it's *Purple and Brown*, it's *Purple and Brown.*"

—What do you mean, who painted the picture? What's that got to do with it? There is more than one purple and more than one brown and it ought to be *Purples and Browns.*

"I painted it, goddamn it, and I say it's *Purple and Brown.*" Olive's voice had risen.

—All right, all right. It's settled. You painted it.

Olive was up early the next morning. She bathed and had breakfast and then straightened up the apartment. At a little after ten o'clock, she left for her studio. It was cold so Olive took the crosstown bus rather than walk through the park.

When Olive reached her studio, she put on her smock. She would do another painting, one along the same lines as *Purple and Brown.* It would be the same kind of painting but she would use a smaller canvas this time. And in this picture, she would use lots of green.

She started blocking out her new canvas. She made some sketches.

Olive worked for several hours. As she was leaving her studio, she remembered the rental library book. She had forgotten to return it this morning as she'd planned. She'd have to go get it now and take it back. No use paying extra money for such a bad novel.

But Olive forgot again when she returned to her apartment.

And she forgot the next day.

She hated herself for forgetting. But of course it was easy to understand why such a stinking book would escape her mind. Besides, she had been busy thinking of her new painting.

On the fourth day after she had finished the book, Olive remembered to take it back. She paid the rental fee. It was her own fault that she had wasted three days' fee on the book. And the book stank!

She was making good progress on her new painting. The colors were lighter and brighter than those in *Purple and Brown.*

As Olive worked, her new painting began to change. She became excited. It was a wonderful thing that was happening, she thought. The painting seemed to take hold of her and to control her brush. This change in her painting must be a sign of a change in her. She was developing and growing. There were times when she found herself resisting this growth and dragging her feet in a way. But she certainly didn't drag her feet because she wanted to.

—Wait a minute, ol' gal.

She must unconsciously want to drag them or else she wouldn't. That stood to good psychoanalysis, and good psychiatry.

But even if she had been guilty of dragging her feet in the past, she was getting to a stage now that would be beyond any of this. She was going in the direction of her painting, a direction that was new and original. This would be the sign of a complete recovery from anything and everything that might have been wrong with her.

After a few more days' work on her picture, Olive felt even more strongly that she was making progress.

One afternoon, after finishing, Olive returned to her apartment. She was thinking about her picture, about her progress. She would not drag her feet this time.

"Don't worry, I won't," Olive spoke aloud.

—I promise you I won't either.

That settled it.

Olive looked around the living room. She was alone.

TEN

Autumn was approaching. Olive was getting dressed to visit her father and Bernice. Sunday night dinners did not bother her as much as they had. She was getting better. She hoped her father would notice how much she had improved.

They were having cocktails.

Olive talked more than usual. But her father didn't seem to notice that she was so much better. Or if he noticed, he didn't care. And if he didn't care, how could she expect Bernice to? But it wasn't just that, their not caring, that struck her as odd. Her father wasn't saying much. He was being unusually quiet. Well, she couldn't allow this to bother her too much. Didn't he know how it pained her when he acted like this? And he shouldn't do anything to distress her. After all, he was her father. He should have some understanding. Did he? Did he have any idea what it meant for him to be her father? She doubted it. Something was wrong tonight. She couldn't put her finger on it, but something was wrong.

By the time the three of them had sat down to dinner, Olive had given up trying to make conversation.

There's something rotten in the State of Armsburg, she thought. She became quiet.

Didn't Olive feel well? Bernice asked. She was eating so little. Olive said that she just wasn't hungry tonight. Couldn't she try to eat a little bit more?

Olive wanted to tell Bernice Ash to mind her own goddamned business.

Instead, she made a pretense at eating more.

—Might as well keep peace in the family.

But she soon gave up; it was too awful trying to get the food down. This Sunday night supper was turning out to be unbearable.

Shortly after they got up from the table, Olive excused herself, saying she was very tired.

Solomon Armsburg tried to put the evening out of his mind. He didn't want Olive to have any more breakdowns. He had already spent thousands of dollars to make her well. This was one of the things that he had intended to talk to her about tonight. Olive was a sick girl. She could never be responsible enough to be given a sizable sum of money, let alone have control over his estate.

It hadn't been easy to come to this decision. Not by a damn sight. She was his only child. But what choice did he have?

She had seemed all right the early part of the evening. Then, for no reason that he could see, she had changed.

Later, he and Bernice had talked about it.

"I can't understand what went wrong tonight," Solomon Armsburg said.

"I know, dear." Bernice was sympathetic.

"I hope it doesn't mean anything, I hope she's not headed for another breakdown."

He fixed himself another brandy.

"More for you, Bernice?"

"No thank you, Solomon."

He sat down again.

"It's a sad thing for a father," Bernice said.

"Yes it is."

"But, Solomon, you know that you've done everything that you could do."

"Yes, I think so."

"Your own conscience can be clear."

"My conscience is clear, Bernice. Thank God for that. I can honestly say I've done my best."

"And what more can any man do, Solomon?"

Solomon Armsburg nodded gravely.

ELEVEN

Olive was too upset about last night to go to her studio. She would not be able to paint. There was no use in trying.

A little after four o'clock, Merton Nydol telephoned. Olive had resolved that she would never ever let him up to her apartment again. She didn't go for rear end drivers.

He can use someone else's back door, she had told herself.

When Merton Nydol asked if he could come up, Olive said yes. He arrived with a bottle of brandy.

Oh, so he thought he could camp for a long time, did he? Well, she'd show him.

As they sat drinking the brandy, Olive watched him warily.

Merton Nydol leaned forward to pour himself a fresh drink.

"Finish up and I'll pour you another one," he offered.

Olive finished her drink.

"Thank you," she mumbled, handing him her glass.

"Well, how have you been?" he asked, pouring her another drink.

"No complaints."

"Good, I'm glad to hear that," he said, sitting down.

"And how have you been?" Olive asked.

He looked at her uncertainly. Then he smiled.

"Come to think of it, I've been feeling pretty good."

He reached for a cigarette. Eying him, Olive decided that he was a particularly unattractive man. Noticing her gaze, Merton Nydol smiled. She smiled back.

She's warming up, he thought.

He's not so bad when he smiles, Olive thought.

She hoped he wouldn't use the back door this time. If he did, she supposed she'd have to let him but she preferred the front door.

Merton Nydol had finished his brandy. She ought to keep up with him. Olive gulped the rest of her drink. She began to cough.

"Take it easy," Merton Nydol said.

After a few moments, Olive was able to catch her breath.

"I'm all right now, I choked on my drink, that's all," she explained.

"You should be careful, my dear."

"Oh I'll never die choking over brandy," Olive laughed.

"I should hope not."

"It would be too foolish, choking to death on brandy."

Olive laughed again. There was something peculiar about her laugh.

"Merton." Her voice was strident.

"Yes?"

"You're neglecting me; I need another drink."

"I neglected myself, too."

"Well you mustn't. You mustn't neglect your little self."

"I won't do it again, I promise."

He poured two more brandys and handed one to Olive.

"Thank you, Merton."

"You're welcome. And now, to no self-neglect," he said, raising his glass and drinking.

"To no neglect of Olive, either," Olive toasted.

"Olive won't be neglected." His look was bold.

Olive became coy.

Merton Nydol walked over and kissed her.

"Oh, no," Olive said, still coy.

"Oh yes, Olive."

"Tired?" Olive asked.

"Not too tired," Merton Nydol said, holding a glass of brandy.

"You're not?"

"Why no; are you?"

"No. But I hurt," Olive answered.

"Hurt? Where?"

"Where do you think I hurt?"

Olive's voice was angry.

Merton Nydol took another sip.

"You can't be fully civilized sexually unless you like Greek love," he said.

"Oh don't hand me that," Olive snapped.

"But I mean it."

He was surprised at her sudden rage.

"What's the matter?" he asked.

"Get out!"

Her voice was hoarse. He looked at her; her face was wild.

"Get out, I say," she shrieked.

Shocked by her fury, he sat, stunned. He didn't know what to say. Olive glared at him.

"I said get out or I'll scream. Get out, you dirty old man. Get out or I'll call the police, do you hear?"

He sat, too shocked to move.

"Get the hell out of my house, I say."

—My God, suppose the neighbors hear her screaming like this and call the cops.

Frantically, he jumped up and lunged for his hat and coat. Stumbling, he banged into the door. There was a sharp pain. He could feel blood running down near his eye.

"Get out, I say."

—She's nuts. Her voice is enough to shrivel a man's spine. Where in hell's the doorknob? I've got to get out of here.

"Get out!"

The blood was streaming down his face from the cut. How badly hurt was he? He couldn't stop to look now, he had to get away from her.

Merton Nydol finally managed to get through the door. He could hear her behind him, still shrieking.

After a short nap, Olive awakened and fixed herself something to eat. As she picked at her food, she thought of her painting. She ought to do a whole series in the same style as *Purple and Brown*. She had wasted a whole day but there was no sense in crying over spilled milk. At least she'd gotten rid of that Merton Nydol.

Would he try to come back?

She got up and checked the front door. Thank God for that double lock.

—You won't get in here again. I'd have to have holes in my head to let you back in. There are no holes in my head. You won't get in here again, mister. That door's going to stay bolted, just the way it is.

Olive sat in the darkness like someone in a stupor.

Olive remained sitting all night. By the time dawn came, she was sneezing and coughing. And by ten o'clock, she was burning with fever. She telephoned her father and told him that she was ill. She sounded almost incoherent over the telephone.

—She must be having another breakdown.

This was what Solomon Armsburg thought as he rushed to his daughter's apartment.

After telephoning her father, Olive had fallen into a feverish sleep. She did not hear the doorbell. Solomon Armsburg rang it for about five minutes. Finally, he tried the superintendent's bell. The superintendent recognized Solomon Armsburg. Together, they rode up to the tenth floor. When the superintendent unlocked Olive's door, Solomon Armsburg saw the blood in the foyer. Alarmed, he called out. There was no answer but he could hear moans coming from the bedroom. He rushed in, the superintendent behind him.

Hearing them, Olive half rose in her bed. Her face was flushed, her eyes wild. She moaned again and began to mumble incoherently.

"What's the matter, Olive?" her father asked.

She mumbled.

"She's sick, Mr. Armsburg," the superintendent said.

Olive looked at her father with pleading eyes. There was terror on her face.

Was she dying? Solomon Armsburg wondered. She was sick, he

could see that. She could die. The thought shook him. It was an unexpected wallop. He had to get a doctor, and fast. Olive had to get to a hospital right away. Her life might be at stake.

Solomon Armsburg rushed back into the living room and called his own doctor, Dr. Kling. Briefly, Solomon Armsburg told him what the situation was. Dr. Kling said he would be right over.

"We've got to get her to a hospital right away," Dr. Kling announced. "I'll phone for an ambulance."

He looked around.

"Where is the telephone?"

"Over there, Doctor," Solomon Armsburg pointed.

Dr. Kling walked over, picked up the receiver and ordered an ambulance. It was an emergency, he said.

Olive's shallow breathing could be heard in the living room. Dr. Kling went back into the bedroom.

In about twenty minutes, the ambulance arrived. Olive was carried out of her apartment on a stretcher.

At the Eastmore Hospital on East Eighty-seventh Street, Olive Armsburg was given antibiotics and placed in an oxygen tent. Dr. Kling told Solomon Armsburg that his daughter was critically ill.

For four days, Olive's life hung in uncertainty. On the fifth day, she began to rally but her improvement was slow. Drained, she lay in bed, mute.

Dr. Lustig visited her every day. He advised Solomon Armsburg that Olive was catatonic and that she should be sent back to the sanitarium as soon as she was strong enough to be moved. Solomon Armsburg accepted Dr. Lustig's recommendation.

When Dr. Kling pronounced Olive well enough to be transferred, Solomon Armsburg authorized her transfer to the sanitarium. On learning that she was to be sent there, Olive whimpered but said nothing. Solomon Armsburg saw the fear in her eyes. But what else could he do? He had no alternative. Olive was sick, mentally sick.

For the third time, Olive Armsburg underwent electric shock treatment.

Several weeks passed. Olive began to look forward to her release. She was still weak and listless because of her bout with pneumonia. This was why, the doctors told her, they were keeping her a little longer this time. Olive did not believe them. She was being punished. They were taking advantage of her because she was too weak to protest. If they'd let her out, she could get back her strength.

Finally, plans were made to release her from the sanitarium. This time, both her father and Dr. Lustig came to get her.

Riding back to Manhattan, Olive felt good. She was happy; she was going to be free again. She had fooled them all by getting well. They had had to let her out. She was going to be a free woman again. She felt good. Why shouldn't she? This was something to feel good about. She had won. Against her father and Bernice put together.

TWELVE

She was home again. She could pick up where she'd left off. Where had she left off? She could remember some things but there were other things that she was not so sure of. How could she pick up where she had left off if she couldn't remember where she had left off? She could remember Merton Nydol but she couldn't remember where she had left off with him. Well, starting right now, she was not going to worry about things she couldn't remember. So much had happened to her, and so fast. She still didn't know what all the shouting had been about.

It didn't matter if she remembered or didn't remember.

Still, it bothered her. Maybe something was wrong with her up there. If they found out she couldn't remember, they might send her back. And she didn't want to go back. But they could make her go back, want to or not. If she could only remember, they couldn't take her back.

But it was no use. She couldn't remember. She tried and tried but it was no use.

Bright sunlight poured through her bedroom window. Olive lay in bed. She would get up, take a shower and dress, have some breakfast, and then go to her studio. To hell with what she couldn't remember.

There was dust everywhere. Olive had scarcely stepped into her studio when she was sneezing and coughing. But the dust gave her something to do. She had suddenly felt the need to do something, something routine. Dusting, sweeping, and mopping her studio would be good for her.

She was exhausted. She had even scrubbed the floor. She couldn't do anything else today.

Olive took a taxi back to her apartment, had a drink, and fell into bed without eating or undressing.

Olive woke up fully clothed. For a moment she was frightened. But then she remembered how she had worked herself into a state of exhaustion. God she had been tired. She still didn't want to get up; she wanted to sleep longer. A long time, like forever, only not forever. But she was dying to see how her studio looked after all that cleaning. She couldn't do both things, go back to sleep and see how her studio looked. Not unless she were two people. And she wasn't two people. She was only one person. She wished she were two.

She was awake now. She put her feet into a pair of mules. She was hungry. She was more than hungry; she was starved. And grimy. And her bladder was full. Her bladder came first.

Olive hurried into the bathroom.

Olive was thrilled at the sight of her work. She had worked like a *shvartze* and the place looked it. Now she would be able to paint. She put on her smock.

But Olive didn't paint. She fussed about the studio some more, arranging and rearranging things.

It was almost three–thirty; too late to paint. The light was too poor to start now. She'd go back to her apartment.

Olive was restless. She didn't know what to do with herself. This was not correct; not precisely correct. She could think of lots of things to do and lots of places to go. But for what?

She fixed herself a martini.

Staring at the gathering darkness through her living room window,

Olive felt sad. The day seemed sad. Maybe the day felt sad like she did. That was a silly thought. Why? Why couldn't the day feel sad? How could anyone know that the day didn't feel sad? No one could know. She was just as right as anyone else was. Nobody could know for sure that the day didn't feel sad. Maybe it did.

Olive turned away from the window.

She ached all over. She had overexerted herself cleaning up the studio. She was still weak. She had been sick for a long time; she had to be careful. Suppose she should have a relapse? She might die.

Frightened, Olive went to bed.

Olive suffered no relapse. She was weak but not ill. It was months before she was strong enough to paint.

THIRTEEN

Now, at long last, she was ready to paint. She had regained her stength. She could start a new week with a new work. This did not mean to say that she had to start on this very day, Monday. She could start tomorrow.

On Tuesday morning, Olive went to her studio. She could start painting now. It had been a long time. Too long.

Olive put on her smock, put a fresh canvas on her easel, took out her pallette and brushes. She was ready now.

She stood before the blank canvas for over an hour. Her mind would not function. She must not be ready to paint yet.

That was it, she wasn't ready. When she was, her subconscious mind would dictate what she should paint. There was no point in trying to force herself. Whatever she did wouldn't be any good.

Olive returned to her apartment.

The next day, Wednesday, Olive went to her studio early. But again, she couldn't work.

She remained lethargic the entire week. This did not bother her. She had neither the energy nor the will to paint, and neither the energy nor the will to worry about her lack of energy or will.

Olive slept a lot.

Gradually, Olive began to think of her painting and of herself. She wanted to do things, exciting things. The doctors had warned her to be careful but how goddamned careful can you get? She wanted to go to a bar. She hadn't yet. She'd been careful for a long time now. One of these days she was going to stop being so goddamned careful. She was going to go out to a bar, have a few drinks,

and bust loose. And when she did, she was going to have a man.
Or maybe more than one man. If she felt like it, she would. It
wouldn't be the first time.

Instead of sitting here thinking about it, she could do it. It was
easy enough. All she had to do was walk out of her apartment and
into a bar. Once there, all she had to do was order a drink. And wait.
Chances were, nine times out of ten, that there would be a man
ready, willing, and able to pick her up. The rest was easy. Birds,
bees, pussy cats knew how to do it. And so did she, goddamn it. It
was too simple for words; but she hadn't kept it simple. She was
up to her ears in it. What was the matter with her? She didn't have
to be afraid to bust out; there was nothing to stop her.

—And goddamn it, nothing will!

Olive dressed and left the apartment. She walked to the corner
and turned right on Central Park West trying to make up her mind
where to go.

After walking a few blocks, she decided to go to a bar on the
east side, on Madison or Lexington Avenue. She'd walk a few blocks
first and then she'd take a cab over.

She continued down Central Park West, all the way down to
Columbus Circle.

It wasn't so long a walk; the blocks were short. It had taken her
less than half an hour and she hadn't walked fast either. She enjoyed
walking. But this was enough.

Olive hailed a cab.

She got out at Fifty-ninth and Lexington. For a moment, she
stood on the corner, undecided. She looked east. Then she started
walking south on Lexington Avenue. She would find a bar along
here. New York was full of bars. She didn't know them all but she
knew a lot of them. She smiled.

She was ready now for a couple of martinis. And for whatever
else would follow.

Olive lifted her glass, took a drink, and looked down at the man giving her the eye from the end of the bar. He might do. Medium-sized, well dressed. Well enough dressed. Middle-aged, not bad looking, friendly enough looking. Yes, he might do. Olive glanced off.

She turned to look at him again. He smiled. She wouldn't smile back, not yet. She took another sip. He was watching her. She smiled.

"Mind if I join you?"

"Not at all," Olive said, casually.

"Would you like another one?"

"I think I would, Jack."

"Then another one you shall have."

His name was Jack Kalish. Olive wondered if she could do better. She looked around. She probably could do better but there was no harm in letting him buy her a martini.

The bartender brought their drinks. Jack put a five-dollar bill on the bar.

"Let's drink to something," he said, picking up his drink.

"All right."

"What'll it be?"

Olive thought for a few seconds.

"Let's drink to whatever happens," she said.

They touched glasses.

"To whatever happens," he said.

They drank.

This was a good bar. The crowd was lively and there was lots of talk. Talk? It was shouting, really, but she liked it. And she was doing her share of it. You had to shout if you wanted to be heard. She was enjoying herself but she could tell that Jack was getting anxious to go.

"What are you going to do now, Olive?" he asked.

"Ask you to get me another martini."

"Would you like another one?"

"That's what I said, isn't it?"

"It's so noisy in here that I wasn't sure."

"Well now you are," Olive smiled.

He frowned.

"We'll leave soon," she promised.

"Yes?"

"Yes, and we'll go to my place."

"I'll order those martinis," Jack Kalish said.

"Come on, Olive, let's go."

"I want another drink," Olive mumbled.

The bar was one big blur to her. Maybe she shouldn't have another drink. What happened to her last one? She didn't remember drinking it. Someone must have knocked it out of her hand or something.

"I wanna . . . "

"What's that?" Jack asked, leaning toward her.

"I wanna . . . "

She was dizzy. She wanted to go home. She swayed against Jack Kalish.

"I wanna go home."

"All right, we'll leave."

"You come home with me," Olive said.

"Yes. I'll take you home."

"You can come to bed . . . "

Olive almost fell. Holding her arm, Jack Kalish led her out of the crowded bar. They staggered toward the curb. A man bumped against Olive and she stumbled again. Jack Kalish waved at a passing taxi. It stopped.

"Here," he said, helping her into the cab.

He got in after her.

She felt awful. She had busted out all right. She had gone out, gotten drunk, picked up a man, and gotten laid. She didn't know how many times. She had been very drunk but she had known what was happening to her. She was getting what she wanted, all right. She must have come four or five times. But then she must have passed out. When she woke up, she was alone and the sun was up. She didn't know for sure what time it was but she knew that it was the morning after. Her head. What a hangover. And her mouth felt dry. She could feel a fever blister starting on her lip. She didn't want to get out of bed. Why hadn't she left her clock on the dresser where she could see what time it was without getting out of bed?

A lot of the night before was blurred but she could remember leaving the bar and riding back here with Jack. Jack Kalish. That was his name, the man she had picked up. She had tried to unlock her door but she hadn't been able to. Jack had taken the key from her hand and had unlocked the door for her. They had no sooner walked in when he had started undressing her. The next thing she knew he was on top of her and he had stayed there for a long time. Not that she was complaining; she had liked it. While it lasted, that is. And while she could remember. Then she had passed out, she supposed, or fallen asleep. What was the difference? One was the same as the other. She was awake now and it was over with.

And she was hung over. God was she hung over.

Olive turned on her side and went back to sleep.

The telephone woke her up. It took her a few seconds to realize that it was the phone that had awakened her. Who could it be? With a curse, she got out of bed to answer it.

It was her father.

Solomon Armsburg had telephoned to ask her to come see him in his office. Then he had asked her how she was feeling. Fine, she told him. When did he want to see her, she asked.

"Can you make it today, Olive?"

"Yes I can."

She promised to be in his office at three. That would give her plenty of time, she thought.

It was only after hanging up that she wondered why her father had called her. She'd have to wait and see. It probably had something to do with her rights to his money. He was going to ask her to sign her rights away, she bet. And she would have to do it. What else could she do? She didn't have the strength to oppose him. She wouldn't know how even if she wanted to. She was helpless. The thought depressed her.

Olive went to the bathroom.

When Olive walked into her father's office, she could tell he was angry. She was fifteen minutes late. She knew that it annoyed him for anyone to be late for an appointment but she couldn't help it. He had no right to get annoyed.

She apologized for being late. He said it was nothing, nothing at all. He put his arms around her and kissed her. Then he asked her to sit down. He asked her how she felt and when Olive told him that she felt fine, he told her that he was glad, very glad to hear it.

It didn't ring true. There was something funny about the way he said it. And the way he pretended not to be angry with her for being late. Something fishy was going on. She'd have to be careful. She didn't want to get balled up now. Her father was acting funny; he wasn't acting right.

"Olive . . ."

The way he said her name sounded a warning.

He paused.

"Olive . . ." he began again.

This is it, she thought.

"I wanted you to come here so that we could talk about something that I hope you'll understand."

"Yes?"

"You've been a very sick girl, Olive."

"I know; but I am getting better now."

"I know you are, my dear. I always knew that you would, too."

A lot he cares, Olive thought.

"Yes, indeed, I'm very happy about the way you're coming along, Olive."

"I am too," Olive mumbled.

Solomon Armsburg felt sad. The tonelessness in her voice distressed him. Olive was still a sick girl. She had improved enough so that she didn't have to be kept in a sanitarium but she had not recovered fully. He really didn't know if she could. But he must not show signs of doubt. He had this painful but necessary business to settle with her. It would be folly not to go ahead as he had planned. The plain fact was that his daughter was not competent.

Solomon Armsburg thought he loved his daughter. He was determined to fulfill his duties and obligations toward her. But she was a burden.

Solomon Armsburg did not love his daughter. He was uneasy about her, but it was no more than that. What he was doing was more unpleasant for him than it was painful. She would have been a heavy emotional burden if he still loved her.

"Olive, I have some papers for you to sign."

"Yes."

Her voice was low and dull.

"I think it's wise for you to sign over your share of family matters."

She nodded. She mustn't let him know how scared she was. He was pushing papers across the desk and handing her a pen.

Olive signed the papers.

"Things won't be any different for you, Olive, you'll still get your check every month."

"I know."

"And here's an extra check for you now in the event that you want to buy yourself some new clothes."

He handed her a check. Olive stared at it before she picked it up.

"Thank you."

He wanted her to leave; she could see that. He had handled this matter and now he was set for other business.

FOURTEEN

Olive left her father's office feeling deserted. She walked dejectedly, a vacant look on her face. She had no idea where she was going; she just walked. Occasionally someone would turn to stare at her but she didn't notice. She kept on going.

She found herself in front of the building where she lived. She hadn't realized she was walking home. Or had she? She entered the lobby and took an elevator up to the tenth floor.

She was home.

It was the first time she had thought of her apartment as "home."

Olive awakened, terrified, in the dark apartment. It took her a few seconds to realize where she was. Then, her terror vanished. But wait a minute.

Was that a sound? There was someone in the apartment. She lay still. If she didn't stir, maybe they would go away. Maybe. But they could hear her breathing. They didn't have to hear her; they could see her.

She trembled. Someone was approaching her in the darkness, coming closer to her bed. She dare not reach out and turn on the lamp. A window pane rattled and the wind ruffled the curtains at her opened window.

—Get out of here. Do you hear me? Get out!

Olive sat up. They wouldn't leave; she knew it.

—Why? Why won't you leave? No one asked you here.

She switched on the lamp.

—Now will you get out?

She couldn't see them but she could still hear them.

—Get out; I don't want you here.

They would not leave.

—What do you mean you don't care whether or not I want you here? It's my apartment, isn't it?

And then.

—Shut up!

She looked around. They weren't in this room; they were somewhere else. She could hear them. They could hide all they wanted to but she knew they were still here. Wait a minute, they were talking again.

—What? What did you say?

Olive tilted her head to listen.

—Oh, so you are leaving. Well, don't come back.

They were gone now. She listened. She could hear nothing. She had gotten rid of them this time.

Olive had fallen asleep again. It was still dark when she woke up. She wished it were morning. She thought of her visit to her father's office. It had been awful. She lay there feeling very sad. In a few moments, she fell asleep again.

The next day, Olive was still depressed. She didn't feel like doing much of anything. And she didn't. She didn't go to her studio.

But on the morning after, she awakened early and in a fury of energy. She cleaned her apartment. When it was all spic and span, she wanted to pitch in and do it all over again. She hadn't felt sad while she was cleaning.

The next morning, Olive woke up happy. As she prepared her breakfast, she thought of her work. Then, after eating, she hurried to her studio. She began a new canvas, a small one.

The day after, she completed it.

She started on another one immediately.

This painting was not as cluttered. And the colors were less foreboding than the heavy purples and deep browns. There was a sense of space in this work. She was getting a new grip on herself, Olive told herself. Her painting was helping her get well. And now that she had signed away her rights to her father's estate, she was no longer Olive Armsburg, heiress. She had to succeed as a painter. She had to become someone.

It was desperation that drove Olive. But she thought it was enthusiasm, and that she was in a new phase, both in her life and in her painting.

This time she was going to get well, absolutely well, she told herself.

FIFTEEN

Olive painted many canvases. She worked fast and even though her colors were less somber and there was more space in her work, distorted organs of the body still appeared frequently.

Olive joined a collective group of artists who showed their work in a small gallery at Seventy-sixth Street and Madison Avenue. There were nine of them. They called themselves The New Group, and the gallery, The New Gallery. Olive was the tenth member. She believed that she needed the contact with younger painters.

It was a friendly group but not quite as friendly as she had hoped. It came as a shock that the younger members considered her an "older" painter. She was middle-aged. To them, middle-aged was old. This stunned her. She knew she was no longer a girl but she never thought about it. Her life was yet to be lived. This was the same way she felt as a young girl. Whatever she did today did not count so much; it was what she would do tomorrow and the day after tomorrow that would really count. Life was tomorrow.

The young artists of The New Group were sad reminders to Olive that she was no longer young. She would have to act her age. Had she been kidding herself all these years? Was she a real nut?

—To hell with it.

She would concentrate on her work.

Olive began to think of exhibiting her work. Any member of The New Group could, once a year. She planned a one-man exhibition.

She had never had a show of her own before. She had pictures hung with others but this time it would be all hers. It could turn out to be the biggest thing in her life.

But it wouldn't be a big thing unless she worked hard. Olive drove herself. She spent hours in her studio every day. She painted with more desperation than before. Often, she painted without thinking. After working this way for an hour or so, she would come to a stop. Her trance would vanish and Olive would take this as her signal to stop for the day.

Olive regarded these trancelike hours as periods of inspiration. There was no other way to interpret them, no other explanation. She was inspired. Her inspiration came from deep within her. That was why she painted as though she were in a trance, her hand moving the brush almost automatically. She was inspired. That was all that mattered.

In three weeks, Olive completed enough paintings, with some to spare, to fill the wall space of The New Gallery. Many of them were good. She could hang them without any feeling of shame.

She was ready now, ready for her big show.

Olive began carrying her paintings to the gallery. She was determined to do this herself. Unless they were too big, she carried them down on foot. She could take only one or two at a time.

Sometimes she got tired and was tempted to hire someone to carry them. But no. She wouldn't. She would rather save the money; she had to be more careful about money now.

Four more days, she thought.

Well, everything was ready.

Olive was spent; her mind barely functioned. She could do nothing but wait for the big day. She wasn't so confident about the show now. Confident? Who in hell was she kidding? She was scared. What would people think about her work. She was putting herself at the mercy of strangers who would come and look. They would judge her and buy or not buy. But she didn't expect to sell many paintings. She didn't know what she expected. Suppose something went wrong? Something would; she just knew it.

Why did she ever get herself into this? She should never have planned this one-man show.

Olive was in a panic.

Olive was eating with her father and Bernice. After dinner, the three of them would go to Olive's opening. Olive nibbled at her food; she was nervous, too nervous to eat much. Her father urged her to try to eat a little, at least, but she told him she couldn't.

He said no more but he couldn't understand how not eating was going to help her show.

Bernice scarcely spoke. She didn't want to distress the girl, not if she could help it. There was always some strain when Olive came over but tonight Olive seemed more tense than usual. She hoped that everything would go all right, for Solomon's sake as much as for Olive's.

The dinner over, they drank brandy. Olive asked for a second one.

The gallery was just a few blocks away. But Olive was impatient; she said she had to get there in a hurry, they couldn't walk. Solomon hailed a cab. During the short ride, Olive bit her nails. When the cab stopped, she jumped out, almost falling.

Seeing his daughter trip, Solomon Armsburg shook his head. Bernice squeezed his hand. Olive rushed inside. Solomon and Bernice followed.

Inside the gallery, Olive stopped. She felt a little dizzy. She stood still for a few seconds. She didn't know what to do. On a table before her, there was a big bowl of Claret punch. Olive went to it, reached for a cut glass, and ladled the punch into it. She took a quick swallow. Solomon and Bernice walked in just as she was taking a second gulp.

Neither Solomon nor Bernice said anything as they looked at the paintings. They didn't know what to say. What could they make of all this? There was nothing in them that they could recognize. And both Solomon and Bernice only liked or disliked paintings in which they could recognize objects, or scenes, or figures. You could like color and color had a lot to do with paintings, but color was different from things. In this way, they dismissed their response to color.

As they walked from canvas to canvas, they began to feel revulsion. Although they could not recognize distinct objects, it seemed to them that there were many organs and parts of entrails in the paintings. They looked at each other. There was understanding in the glance they exchanged. This was just too bad. Solomon was pained that his daughter should have painted such pictures. Why had she wanted to exhibit this stuff? He looked at Bernice again, shaking his head.

Seeing these paintings by the daughter of her husband, a man so kind and generous, made Bernice realize that she could never like the girl. She had tried to understand her but she couldn't. Oh how her Solomon must be hurt.

Olive had had two glasses of punch.

She wished her father and Bernice hadn't come. It was stupid to wish that now.

She went to the punch bowl again. She drank half of another glass of punch and then turned around. About twenty-five people had come. Some were talking and others moved slowly about. She watched her father and Bernice. They were still looking at her paintings. She could tell that they didn't like them. How could she expect them to? They couldn't understand what she had been doing. This shouldn't upset her but it did. If they tried to understand, they could. They had no desire to. They didn't care; that was what was so unforgivable.

Olive finished her third glass of punch and poured herself another. She went over to her father and Bernice. She had to be careful; she had to walk straight.

"Well, Olive," her father said, "this is quite an exhibition."

"Do you like it, Father?"

The minute the words were out, Olive wished she hadn't said them.

"I'm interested, let me put it that way, Olive."

"Well if you're interested, it would seem to me that you would have an opinion."

"Not necessarily, Olive."

She looked at him, her expression quizzical.

He didn't like the way she was staring at him. She was trying to intimidate him. Best to ignore the look, or at least pretend to.

"Why can't I be interested, Olive, but perhaps not know enough to make judgments."

"Oh skip it, Solomon."

This was the first time that Olive had ever called her father "Solomon." She was tense for a few seconds.

Nothing happened. He didn't react. She was standing here expecting the world to cave in and he hadn't even noticed. To hell with him.

Olive drained her glass.

"Excuse me," she said, moving past them to greet a heavyset man who had just entered the gallery.

Solomon and Bernice watched her. They didn't know what to think.

Olive gave her hand to the heavyset man.

He was not very attractive, Bernice thought. Solomon looked at the man, too. He didn't think much of the fellow. But then what could you tell about a man at one glance? He turned to Bernice. She smiled at him.

"I don't understand the paintings, Sol."

"Neither do I."

"I didn't know what to say to her," Bernice said, "I didn't want to hurt her feelings."

"I know," he said, squeezing her hand.

His name was Tom Shapleman. Olive had picked him up in a bar, taken him home, and gone to bed with him. He had told her that he liked her paintings, and had said that if she should ever have an exhibition, she should let him know. He had intimated, or so Olive had interpreted, that he might be interested in buying one. Olive had taken his address and had promised that she would.

"Here I am."

This was how Tom Shapleman greeted Olive.

Olive followed while he looked at her paintings. It didn't take her long to realize that they were not his dish of tea. At one point, he even shook his head as if he were trying to clear it. To hell with him, let her pictures make him dizzy.

"Gee, Olive, I didn't know you painted this kind of . . . pictures."

"You've seen my work before, Tom."

He turned back to the canvas.

"Come on, let me take a closer look."

Olive stood beside him. Why had she invited him?

"What does that one mean?" he asked, pointing.

"It means what you see," Olive snapped.

"Well I must be pretty dumb; I don't know what I'm seeing."

"You're seeing an expression of me," Olive said.

She shouldn't have said it; she could tell by the expression on his face.

"I'm a little bit old-fashioned about some things," he said.

"Well . . ." Olive began, but she fell silent.

What was the use? He wouldn't understand. Besides, she had already forgotten what she was going to say. But he wouldn't have understood it so what difference did it make? There she was, on the wall, all of her, pulled apart and put back together again and Tom Shapleman didn't know what her pictures were all about.

Tom Shapleman didn't stay long. The pictures bothered him. When he left, Olive went back to the punch bowl.

She was ashamed. She was staggering but she couldn't help it; she couldn't walk a straight line. She'd have to. She couldn't let all these people know that she was drunk at her own opening. She wasn't really drunk; it was simply a matter of her legs being affected. Her head was still clear. That hadn't been affected by the punch. In fact, she could have another glass. Her head was all right. She would just have to remember to walk more carefully.

Olive got herself another glass.

Both Solomon and Bernice could see that Olive was drunk. Solomon felt helpless but this was not a new feeling. It had become one of his most usual reactions to Olive since he had accepted the fact that she was crazy. Or psychotic, whatever you wanted to call it. He had given up. What else could he do? It wasn't easy. How could it be easy for a man to give up on his only daughter? It was the most painful thing he had ever endured. And humiliating. Thank God for Bernice. He had finally reconciled himself about Olive. He could only feel pity for her. He was sorry for her but any love he had felt was now part of his memory of her. It was part of his loss, the loss of former years. Still, he didn't like seeing her drunk. It was unpleasant. And it hurt. Well, there was absolutely nothing he could do about Olive except spend whatever money necessary to keep her comfortable. There was nothing else he could do.

He looked at her. She was very drunk. He wanted to leave. Her pictures bothered him. He turned to Bernice and said he thought they ought to be leaving.

She had been waiting for this word from him.

SIXTEEN

Eddie Ryan arrived at the gallery. Olive staggered up to him and said that she wanted him to meet her father. Eddie reminded her that he had met Solomon Armsburg a few years back. Olive and her son, Roy, were living with him at the time. He and Phyllis had gone to the Armsburg apartment to pick up their son, Tommy, after a birthday party for Roy.

Oh yes, Olive remembered the party. And she remembered Eddie and Phyllis calling for Tommy but she didn't remember Eddie and her father meeting. It had only been an introduction, Eddie said. Oh, said Olive, as she led him over to where Solomon and Bernice stood.

Solomon Armsburg said he was glad to meet Eddie, he'd heard about him from his daughter. And he had heard of his work, of course, but then most people knew the name Edward A. Ryan, he supposed.

There was a silence.

Solomon Armsburg went on to say that it was an interesting occasion.

Eddie nodded agreement.

Another silence.

"Olive is gifted," Eddie said.

"Yes, I think so, but I'm not used to all this," Solomon Armsburg said, pointing to the canvases.

"It takes getting used to," Eddie commented.

Solomon nodded. Eddie noticed Olive's stepmother listening.

"It's an inner world that Olive is trying to paint," Eddie explained.

He saw Olive floundering near the punch bowl. She was drunk. And pathetic. It was heartbreaking, he thought. And her painting made her more pathetic but it would be cruel to say it.

"I'd enjoy talking to you more, Mr. Ryan, about Olive's pictures; but I don't know if I can do so now; we were leaving."

"Yes, Sol, we must be going," Bernice said.

Solomon nodded and turned to Eddie.

"Yes, we must be leaving; otherwise, I would like to continue this talk."

"Yes," Eddie said, implying that he understood.

They shook hands. Bernice said goodbye and the two of them walked over to say goodbye to Olive. When she saw them, Olive tried to straighten up. Her father thanked her for inviting them and congratulated her on her exhibition. Bernice briefly echoed him.

In a few minutes they were gone.

She knew him but she'd forgotten his name.

"Maybe if I took you home," the man was saying.

They were standing near the punch bowl. Olive looked at him but didn't answer.

Eddie Ryan, who had been watching her out of the corner of his eye, decided that it was time to get her home. He walked over.

"I'm going to take you home now, Olive," Eddie said.

Olive mumbled. The man gave Eddie a surly look but Eddie ignored it.

"Stanley," Olive said.

"Stanley Lester," the man said.

"My name is Ryan," Eddie said.

"Edward A. Ryan," Olive said.

"I've heard of you, Mr. Ryan," Stanley Lester told him.

Ignoring him, Eddie turned to Olive.

"I think you ought to go home now, Olive."

"Yes?"

She could hardly stand; her eyes were glazed.

"How will you get home?" Stanley Lester asked.

"I'll see that she gets home," Eddie said.

"Oh?"

The three of them stood, Olive wavering from side to side.

"Well . . ." Stanley Lester began.

"I'm glad to have met you, Mr. Lester," Eddie interrupted.

"And I'm glad to have met you, Mr. Ryan."

"All right, Olive, I'll get your coat now," Eddie said.

"Good night, Olive. And congratulations," Stanley Lester said.

"Good night," Olive mumbled.

Eddie took her arm and led her across the floor of the gallery. He helped her with her coat, found her purse, and left with her. As they stepped outside, a cab passed.

"Taxi!" Eddie called.

The cab stopped and Eddie helped Olive in. She turned toward him and mumbled something but Eddie couldn't understand what she was saying.

A poor spectacle, Eddie thought.

But there had been times when he had been a worse spectacle and he knew it. He should be more sympathetic than disgusted. But it wasn't disgust that he felt. It was more a feeling of unseemliness.

The cab stopped in front of Olive's building. Eddie paid the driver and helped Olive out. She almost fell but he caught her. He led her toward the lobby. What would the elevator man think? It didn't matter. He walked slowly so that Olive would not seem as drunk as she was. It did matter; not for him but for Olive.

When they got out of the elevator, Eddie asked Olive for her key.

"It's in my purse."

Eddie took her purse, found the key, and opened the door. Olive lurched through the door, staggered over to a table, and switched on a lamp.

"I think you'd better get to bed, Olive."

She stood before him, wavering, a foolish grin on her face.

"Come on, I'm going to put you to bed."

Taking her by the arm, he led her into the bedroom. He switched on the light.

"Just a minute," he said, taking off his coat and dropping it on a chair.

"All right, you're going to bed now," he said firmly.

He removed her coat and placed it on a chair.

"Where's your nightgown, Olive?"

"I don't want it," she mumbled.

"All right, you don't have to wear it. Here, let me help you take off your dress."

Olive lifted her arms. He unzipped her dress and then eased it up over her head. Olive stood, docile. Eddie folded the dress and laid it over the back of the chair.

"Sit down on the bed, Olive."

She obeyed, like a child. Eddie took off her shoes, unhooked her stockings, and pulled them off.

In a few minutes, she stood before him, naked.

"Now, Olive, into bed."

He reached over and pulled the cover down.

"Here, sit down and give me your feet."

She sat on the edge of the bed. Gently, Eddie lifted her feet and placed them under the cover. Then he pulled the covers up, bent over, and kissed her.

"Sleep, Olive, sleep," he said softly.

He went into the kitchen, got a glass of cold water, and returned to the bedroom.

"I'm leaving a glass of water on the stand by your bed, Olive."

She muttered.

"I'm going now."

He kissed her once more and left.

SEVENTEEN

The next morning at about eleven-thirty, Eddie Ryan called to ask Olive how she felt. She said that she was fine; she didn't remember everything but she did remember that he had brought her home and she wanted to thank him. He told her it was nothing; there had been many times when he himself had been that way. He would see her soon. Yes, Olive said, she would like that.

Olive sounded very meek.

Olive remembered little of what had happened. She must have done something horrible. Well, she couldn't remember. It was probably just as well.

Olive did very little painting the next week. But this was natural. After so sustained and prolonged a period of work, there would be something wrong with her if she didn't let up. It was natural that she should slow down after the intensity of the last three weeks. The fact that she wasn't working shouldn't worry her. And she felt about the same as she would feel if she were painting. Her thoughts would come and go just the way they were doing now. There was no point in getting upset. She would paint just as soon as that something inside told her to. When she said something inside she did not mean one of the voices that sometimes told her what to do. Those voices were different; she didn't have to do what they told her to do. She told those voices to shut up. They weren't the same thing as that special something inside that told her to paint. It was different from the voices. The voices talked to her mostly at night. They would wake her up and wouldn't let her go back to sleep. The something inside her was different; it was her inspiration that told her to paint. And when it did, she would. She would pitch in the way she had before her exhibition.

She would listen to that special something inside her; it was different from those voices that kept her awake all night chattering.

Olive woke up. Goddamn them, they were at it again.

—Shut up!

Olive rubbed her eyes and sat up.

—I said, shut up, goddamn it!

—I will not. Go move your own goddamned bowels.

Olive switched on the lamp by her bed.

—Shut up, goddamn it.

She looked around. They sounded like a bunch of monkeys in the zoo. She knew they were there, all right, even if they did hide from her. She didn't have to see them; she could hear their goddamned chatter.

—Go away, I said.

They wouldn't go away and she knew it. How many times had she asked them to go so she could get some sleep? How many times had she ordered them to go? Begged them? But they wouldn't; they didn't want her to sleep any sweet sleep.

—You're ruining my sleep, goddamn it. Go away!

She was wasting her time telling them to leave. She knew that.

—Get out!

They wouldn't get out. They were here for the night. Wasn't that just her luck? Olive leaped out of bed. With her nightgown falling off one shoulder, she glared around the room.

—All right, you win. Stay if you insist but shut up!

It was chilly. She shivered. She picked up her bathrobe off the chair and put it on. Where were her slippers? Oh there they were under the bed. She stuck her feet into them.

—Will you be quiet? Please!

If only they'd listen to her. She looked for a cigarette. There was a pack on her dresser. She walked over, took a cigarette, and put it

in her mouth. Now for a match. Oh there's a book of matches on
the floor. She picked it up and lit her cigarette. Puffing, she glared
at the corners of the room.

—All right. Now that I'm up and awake, you've decided to keep
quiet. Right?

She tilted her head and waited. Then she laughed.

—Go to hell. All of you!

In a few minutes, Olive snuffed out her cigarette and went back
to bed. She fell asleep quickly.

In less than an hour, she was awake again.

—Goddamn it!

They were at it again. What could she do?

—Shut up!

She waited. They were back for the rest of the night; she could
tell.

She felt lousy. She had hardly slept all night. Something kept her
awake but she couldn't remember what. It must have been something important. Odd how her mind was blank. She couldn't remember.

Olive stood by her bed, still in her nightgown, with her hair
disheveled. She stared around the room as though she were looking
for something. She was looking for something. She was looking for
her memory. She didn't see anything that would help bring it back.

—So what?

The matter was settled. It was settled by not being settled. She
would go on to something else. What was next? She didn't care
what it was; she didn't feel like doing it. What didn't she feel like
doing? She didn't feel like doing whatever it was that was supposed
to be next for her.

She was going back to bed. She was tired.

Olive slept until noon. She woke up, still weary. She lay there ar-

guing with herself. She didn't want to get out of bed. But she ought
to get up. Why? There was nothing she had to do. There was no
reason to get up if she didn't want to get up.

Olive fell asleep again.

It was almost five o'clock and getting dark outside when Olive
woke up again. The day was practically wasted.

—So what? Let it waste some more.

Olive slept again.

It was after six when she awakened. She was hungry, hungry as
a horse. Maybe she was as hungry as two horses.

She went to the bathroom; then to the kitchen.

It was past seven. The day was gone. Wasted time was like wasted
money. That's what her father would say. Time thrown away was
like money thrown away because time was money.

Now that she had wasted the day, what was she going to do with
the night? Was she going to waste that, too?

—Here we go again.

She sat and waited. But she didn't know what she was waiting
for. There was nothing to wait for. Nothing was going to happen.
She ought to know that much, at least. You expect something to
happen, get yourself all set for it, and then nothing does happen.
That was enough to disappoint anybody. You don't have to be crazy
to be disappointed in that.

What was she going to do?

Well, she might as well get dressed. Olive went into the bathroom
and soaked herself in a warm bath.

Naked, Olive walked around the apartment. If she did this for
long, she'd catch cold. And who wanted to catch a cold? She put
on her robe. She could hear the wind. It was cold outside. She could

often hear the wind up here. That was because she was high up, on the tenth floor.

—That's it.

That was it. That was the answer. There was something special about the wind in New York. What? What was so special about the wind in New York? What was it that had crossed her mind a minute ago? She couldn't remember. It couldn't have been very important if she didn't remember it. Oh well, she had slept most of the day. The night was ahead. She would have to think of something to do.

Olive was reading. She'd decided that she'd better get at the accumulation of magazines and newspapers stacked in her bedroom. Then she could throw them out. She didn't want to get rid of them before she went through them. She had paid for them; she should at least look at them. After all, she had wasted the day and time was money. She didn't want to waste more.

Olive read herself to sleep.

EIGHTEEN

Olive still saw Dr. Lustig regularly. She went twice a week unless there was some crisis and she became badly disturbed; then she saw him more frequently. Dr. Lustig told Olive she was improving. Olive believed him. She seemed to be getting over her illness. She didn't like to think of it as "illness" but she knew that it was. She was getting better, but she would need all of her morale to recover all the way. And it wasn't good for her morale not to admit she'd been sick.

Olive wanted desperately to believe she was getting well.

Dr. Lustig was aware of Olive's needs. She was an ambulatory psychotic and a manic depressive. She was also compulsive-obsessive and had paranoid tendencies. Olive had had a number of electric shock treatments. Dr. Lustig was convinced that without these, Olive would still be institutionalized. She had been restored to some life in society. He had no way of knowing what the permanent effect of these shock treatments would be, but he was doing the best that could be done for her. He could not perform or achieve miracles.

Dr. Lustig had no qualms about charging Solomon Armsburg thirty-five dollars an hour for treating his daughter. He was, in fact, planning to raise the fee to fifty dollars an hour, but he was waiting for an opportunity to talk to Mr. Armsburg and explain why he should do this. Armsburg had the money; there should be no problem. And the man didn't know what to do about his daughter. He did know that if he were to switch doctors, the change could provoke a crisis for Olive. Not that he, as a doctor, would trade on this. But the facts were the facts. And the fact was that Olive Armsburg was a very sick girl. Another fact was that Solomon Armsburg had

so much money that he didn't have to worry about where he would
find the fifty dollars an hour to pay for his only daughter's treatment.

Having decided to raise Olive's fee, Dr. Lustig waited for an aus-
picious occasion. No such occasion occurred. He decided that to
wait any longer would be to deprive himself of an extra fifteen dollars for each of Olive's visits. He telephoned Mr. Armsburg and
asked if he minded dropping in at his office; he wanted to have a
short talk with him. Solomon Armsburg's voice sounded worried.
He said that of course, if Dr. Lustig wished to see him, he would
go to his office whenever Dr. Lustig suggested. Dr. Lustig suggested the next morning. Solomon Armsburg agreed; then, pausing, he
asked if Olive would be there. Dr. Lustig said that no she wouldn't
be, this was a matter that he wanted to discuss with Mr. Armsburg
privately.
    "Oh!"
    Still worried, Solomon Armsburg said he would be at Dr. Lustig's
office at ten o'clock the next morning.

    Solomon Armsburg arrived at Dr. Lustig's office on time. On
principle, Dr. Lustig kept him waiting for fifteen minutes.

    The Armsburgs had been watching television when the telephone
rang. Solomon Armsburg was surprised by Dr. Lustig's call and his .
first reaction was one of worry. Dr. Lustig must have bad news or
he would not have telephoned and asked him to come see him.
    After hanging up, Solomon talked to Bernice about the call.
    Bernice asked him what Dr. Lustig had to say. He told her that
Dr. Lustig wanted to see him. What about, Bernice wanted to know.
He didn't say, and he hadn't asked, Solomon answered. Bernice said
it was too bad he hadn't asked. Solomon nodded; he should have

thought to ask but he hadn't. He would know soon, though, he had made an appointment to go see Dr. Lustig in his office the next morning at ten o'clock. He figured that it was bad news so it would be better to get it in the morning. Maybe so, Bernice said, but she would have asked if it had been she. But he wouldn't have to wait long, only until tomorrow morning, and it was probably just as well not to know the bad news in advance. That was what he had thought, Solomon said. It might be the best way to think, Bernice told him. Anyway, he would know the next morning.

The Armsburgs went back to watching television. They did not talk for a while; then, during a commercial, Solomon wondered aloud what it was that Dr. Lustig wanted to see him about. The best thing to do, Bernice said, was to try not to worry about it, to wait until he saw the doctor in the morning. He wasn't worrying, he said, just wondering what it was about. It must be serious or else Dr. Lustig wouldn't have telephoned and asked him to go down. Probably, agreed Bernice, but she didn't want to see him worrying, that was what concerned her. Oh well, he wasn't worrying; she could be sure on that score. She was glad of that, Bernice said. Oh no, he knew enough to know that worry didn't get you anywhere. He just hoped there was nothing new wrong with Olive. She hoped so, too, Bernice said.

They went on looking at television. A little later, Bernice said she had kind of a suspicion that it might be money that Dr. Lustig wanted to talk about. This thought had crossed his mind, too, Solomon said, but he didn't think so. Well, maybe, Bernice said, but she had kind of a feeling that it might be.

As he waited in Dr. Lustig's office, Solomon Armsburg thought that it might be money at that. Well, there was no use in speculating about it now. He would be seeing Dr. Lustig soon and he would know definitely. But the appointment had been made for ten and it was almost quarter past. He didn't like being kept waiting this way. He'd made it a point to be on time. But perhaps Dr. Lustig had a reason for being held up, a good one.

Before he could think further on the matter, Solomon Armsburg heard his name being called by the nurse. He could go in now, she told him.

As Solomon Armsburg entered his office, Dr. Lustig stepped from around his desk with his right hand extended to shake hands. He apologized for having kept him waiting and asked him to please sit down. Solomon Armsburg sat facing the desk and Dr. Lustig returned to his chair behind it.

He would come straight to the point, he said. The reason he had asked Solomon Armsburg for this visit was to discuss Olive's fees.

Bernice was right, Solomon thought.

Dr. Lustig said that he was raising the fee to fifty dollars an hour. Sparring for time, Solomon Armsburg said that he thought that was pretty stiff, wasn't it? It might seem so, Dr. Lustig said, but the fact was that he had people on his waiting list who were ready and willing to pay him fifty dollars an hour. Solomon Armsburg did not think Dr. Lustig would say this if it were not true. He agreed to the new fee. They shook hands again and Solomon Armsburg walked out.

He had meant to ask about Olive's condition but he had forgotten.

Olive had an appointment with Dr. Lustig on the same day. This was why Dr. Lustig had asked Mr. Armsburg to come at ten o'clock in the morning. Solomon Armsburg was Olive's legal guardian. Consequently, it was proper that he consult Mr. Armsburg first rather than Olive. She had nothing to do with the handling of money matters. However, Olive should be informed and he planned to do this. He would tell her that her fee had been raised. He could not leave it to her father or to her stepmother and sooner or later, one or the other of them might tell her. His influence with Olive could be impaired if this occurred and he had no intention of permitting that to happen.

Olive arrived a few minutes before her twelve o'clock appointment. The nurse asked her to please wait, the doctor would see her in a few minutes.

Dr. Lustig was with another patient, a young man named Abel

Blaustein who had a girl pregnant and was resisting her attempts to force him into marriage. This was the fourth time Abel Blaustein had been in such a predicament but he had not told Dr. Lustig of the previous occasions.

Dr. Lustig was listening, his eyes on the clock.

At twelve, Dr. Lustig told Abel Blaustein that that would be all for the day. He picked up his pen and started writing as Abel Blaustein rose to leave. Dr. Lustig did not seem to notice that Blaustein was leaving his office but this was a trick of his. He almost always watched his patients leave.

After Abel Blaustein left, Dr. Lustig picked up the phone and told the nurse to send in Miss Armsburg. He put down the phone and arranged the papers on his desk. He sat, composed, waiting for Olive.

There was a rap on the door.

"Come in," he called.

The door opened and Olive, looking harassed, entered.

"But they won't let me sleep, Dr. Lustig."

"Who won't let you sleep?"

"I don't know who they are."

He remained composed at the desk, waiting. A minute passed. That minute of silence would cost Solomon Armsburg almost a dollar, he thought.

"I don't know who they are," Olive repeated, tonelessly.

"What do they look like?"

"I don't know; I can't see them, I only hear them."

"And these voices keep you awake?"

"Yes," Olive nodded.

"What do they say?"

Olive was silent for another dollar's worth.

"I'll try to remember."

"Take your time, Olive."

Finally: "I can't remember but they make such a damned racket that they keep me up."

"Do you do anything?"

"Yes, I tell them to shut up."

Her voice was no longer toneless.

"Do they curse?" Dr. Lustig asked.

"Yes, and I curse them right back but they're not afraid of me."

He waited for her to go on.

"I really do hear them, Dr. Lustig, a lot of voices."

"Is there any particular thing they talk about, or do they try to tell you what to do?"

"I wouldn't if they did."

"Do they try?"

"No."

She looked around the office; her face became confused. She turned back toward him.

"I masturbated myself to sleep."

"Yes?"

"It was the only way I could get to sleep with all the racket they were making."

"And that permitted you to get to sleep?"

"Not right away but after a while it did."

She looked at him, waiting.

"And what else?" he asked.

"I don't know; I don't know that there was anything else."

"Do you remember anything that the voices said?"

Olive's face went blank again. She didn't speak for a moment. Then: "They laughed at me."

"Did they say why?"

"No but I know. It was because I masturbated with my fingers." She looked at him, her face hostile.

"They said I couldn't get anything up me but my fingers. I told them to shut up, that if they didn't, I'd get up, get dressed, go out, and come back with a man who would stick something else up there. They kept laughing so finally I did just that but they didn't come back to watch."

"You've had insomnia before, Olive."

"But this wasn't insomnia. I was so tired and they wouldn't let me sleep," Olive protested.

"Well, you've been unable to sleep before. Was it because of these voices?"

"Yes," she answered meekly.

"And now they won't let you sleep again?"

"It seems that way," she said, her voice still meek.

"You *can* sleep, Olive."

Her eyes opened quickly.

"I can stop them?"

"You did, didn't you?"

"Yes," she answered, surprised.

"You did. And if you can stop them one way, perhaps you can another way."

She looked at him, waiting for him to tell her how. He remained silent.

"What other way?" she asked.

"What other way for what? What do you mean, Olive?"

She looked at him, confused.

"What other way that I can sleep?"

"You can sleep, Olive."

"How?"

"By not hearing the voices; you don't have to hear them."

"But I do," she snapped.

She looked at him, her face apprehensive. He gave no indication that he had heard the hostility in her voice.

"Oh Dr. Lustig, I didn't know what I was saying," she apologized.

"What do you think now, Olive?"

She didn't answer. She moved her lips as if to speak but she didn't. She turned her head away.

"I didn't mean what I said, Dr. Lustig."

"But what if you did mean it?"

"But I didn't."

"But if you did mean it, Olive, you now see that you were wrong and you couldn't mean it again. Isn't that a better way to look at it?"

He spoke softly.

"You're right, Dr. Lustig. That's what I think but I couldn't say it until you put the right words in my mouth."

She laughed.

"Oh Dr. Lustig, I don't know what's the matter with me. Sometimes I feel normal and sometimes I don't. I feel normal now."

He waited for her to go on.

"It's clear to me now; I was having hallucinations."

"That's very good, Olive, go on."

But Olive did not go on. Dr. Lustig waited.

"Suddenly I'm blank; I don't have anything to say."

"Perhaps you've said enough for today."

Olive nodded.

"Olive, I think you can see in this session that you have been making some real progress."

She nodded. She had hoped he would say something like this to her some day. It made her feel wonderful.

"Now, Olive," he went on, "there are only a few minutes of your time left and I want to tell you of a practical matter."

"Yes?"

"It's simply this. I have found it necessary to raise your fee. I have spoken to your father about this and he agrees. It's a settled matter. It changes nothing. It simply means that I am going to be able to continue to give you all the time that is needed."

"Oh that's all right," she said, her voice toneless.

Her exhilaration was gone.

"Now, Olive, I'd like to see you tomorrow. Three o'clock is the only hour that I have free. I would like you to come then."

He leaned forward to make a notation in his appointment book.

"All right, Dr. Lustig, I'll be here."

He looked at her. She smiled thinly.

"Very good, Olive, I'll see you here then at three o'clock."

"Goodbye, Dr. Lustig."

"Goodbye, Olive."

When Olive left, he picked up the phone on his desk.

"I made an appointment with Miss Armsburg for three o'clock tomorrow afternoon," he told his nurse.

NINETEEN

She was home again, if you could call a tenth-floor apartment home. She didn't think she could but it was where she lived.

Suddenly, Olive stood up. What was that? She waited, her body tense. Please, no, she didn't hear anything. Please. A second passed. There were no voices. Her dread vanished. She sat down and lit a cigarette. If Dr. Lustig could help her this much, let him have his fifty dollars an hour. Her father could afford it.

TWENTY

She felt edgy. She had been going to Dr. Lustig four times a week for the past two weeks. Sometimes she would talk a lot, saying all kinds of things. Then, the next visit, she would scarcely talk. She couldn't seem to do anything about these moods; she couldn't lift herself out of them. She felt so helpless; it was terrible.

Once such moods passed, Olive could not remember much about them. And yet she couldn't forget them. She was afraid. She carried her fear within; she was never free of it.

Something awful was going to happen; she knew it.

Olive was helpless in the face of the terror within her. She stopped going to the studio.

She could not go on this way; she would have to pull herself together. She would spend a quiet afternoon with a book, maybe the book Eddie Ryan gave her when she dropped in on him the other night. She had enjoyed the evening, not that Eddie had said much. She had taken a bottle. Eddie was busy writing when she arrived and he went on working. She sat and drank. A little later, he made coffee for her. They talked. Then he took her downstairs and put her in a taxicab. He kissed her on the cheek. She liked to see Eddie Ryan; he wasn't nervous around her. He didn't act as if he were afraid of what she might do.

She would read the book he had given her. It would be good for her to spend a quiet afternoon with a book.

Olive sat, staring at the pages in front of her. Nothing seemed familiar. She couldn't remember where she had left off.

—Jesus Christ!

In a moment.
—No I am not talking to you. Shut up!
—I will not shut up.
—You will shut up when I tell you to shut up!
—I will not.
"You ought to; you don't say a goddamn thing."
—Well all you do is tell me to shut up.
—That's because I want you to shut up.
—Is that all you know how to say?
—To you, it is.

The days dragged on. They were days of suffering for Olive. She tried desperately to cling to reality. She could no longer hope; she didn't have the energy; she was tired. She could not keep her mind from wandering. She would accept whatever thoughts came to her. It didn't matter much what they were; she couldn't remember them. And when you came right down to it, she really didn't care. To hell with it. It wasn't her fault. She wasn't to blame. She had been done in; done in by life.

Olive was losing herself. She had been for years. And now she was disintegrating. She was less in the world than she had ever been. And her health was undermined. Olive had been afraid to go to medical doctors, afraid that they would discover something wrong with her. Neither her father nor Dr. Lustig thought to urge her and left her to her own initiative. Olive didn't go. She knew she should; she sometimes had severe pains in the abdominal region, and occasionally in her chest.

Olive did not miss the studio or her painting. Her painting was like other forgotten parts of her life. Much of what Olive had lived and experienced was becoming deadened to her. A great vacancy about her past was forming in her mind. Her past was far away and it was slipping farther. With her past falling away, she did not suffer tormenting memories. She began to have periods of dreamy softness. She became lazy. She let things go. She neglected herself and her apartment. She would sit for hours, hardly moving, letting pleasant thoughts float through her mind.

She began to drink more. She liked to sip brandy as these pleasant thoughts drifted through her mind.

Olive still went out at night. But when she did, she drank so much that on the next day, she was unable to remember how she had gotten home. She had bumps and bruises on her body but she could not remember if she had fallen down, or if someone had hit her, or what. On some mornings she woke up with painful bruises, her head throbbing, her eyes bleary, her mouth dry, with sharp pains in her abdomen, and with no memory of what had happened. She cried in dread. She felt helpless. There was no end to her agony or terror. Olive did not know what was happening to her.

One night, around midnight, Olive was stricken with severe abdominal pains. She had been asleep. The pain had awakened her. She sobbed. All she could do was cry for help. The room was dark. Olive lay moaning.

Finally, she managed to make a telephone call to her father. He dressed and took a cab to her apartment. The night elevator man let him in. This time it was worse than the other time. He could see that Olive was in danger. The thing to do was to get her to a hospital. He called his doctor who in turn called for an ambulance.

Olive was almost unconscious by the time she arrived at Eastmore Hospital. An examination showed that she had a bleeding ulcer. An emergency operation was recommended. Solomon Armsburg called for the finest surgeon available. In less than two hours, Olive was on the operating table.

The operation lasted six hours.

Olive was very weak. She slept poorly and had to be given sedatives frequently. In the beginning, this did not cause her father undue worry. After all, she had had a major operation. A large part of her stomach had been removed. Of course she was weak.

But as time passed and Olive lay in bed with no visible increase of energy, Solomon Armsburg began to worry. What was going to happen to her? What was to be done? She couldn't live alone now. And he didn't want to take her home. His first duty was to Bernice. It would do none of them any good. And yet something had to be done about her.

Solomon Armsburg talked it over with Bernice. And then with Olive.

It was agreed. Olive would go to her own apartment. Until she was strong enough to take care of herself, feed, bathe, and clothe herself, she would have a practical nurse staying with her. Through Dr. Lustig, Solomon Armsburg was able to get such a nurse, one who had also had experience in handling ambulatory psychotics. Her name was Gladys Walton. She was a formidable-looking woman with shoulders like those of a lady wrestler. After meeting her, Solomon Armsburg told Bernice that he wouldn't want to meet that Gladys Walton in a dark alley. He then described her. Bernice thought that this was good; Olive needed someone big and strong to take care of her.

Gladys Walton moved in with Olive. Olive didn't like it but she knew she had to have someone with her. And Gladys was big and strong. With her around, she wouldn't have to do anything. Her meals would be prepared and served to her.

In the hospital, Olive had been afraid that she would fall. She had once, in the corridor outside her room. This had frightened her. And once her fear had started, it had gotten worse. Her fear of falling became so bad that she dreaded trying to walk.

Olive's weakened condition seemed chronic. She went on from day to day with no signs of change. As time passed, she became adjusted to her weakness. At times she was even afraid that she might grow strong. Olive knew that she would be as helpless in her world with her strength regained as she was now. And at least now, nothing could happen to her. Gladys was here.

By the time Gladys had been with her for two weeks, Olive began to improve. Gladys dispelled some of her hallucinations. Olive
felt safer. She seemed to gain in strength and in energy. She could
move about more, even go out as long as Gladys was with her. But
she still looked gaunt and haggard. She had lost considerable weight
and there were dark circles under her eyes.

On Sunday night, after Olive had been home for almost three
weeks, she went to have dinner at her father's home. Gladys ac-
companied her. Neither Solomon nor Bernice had seen Olive for
two weeks.

They were both appalled by the way Olive looked when she entered their living room. Their shock was plainly revealed to Olive
and she winced. They managed to recover their self-control but it
was too late. To Olive, the look on their faces had been the signal
of her doom.

Solomon, trying to smile naturally, walked toward her and kissed
her on her forehead. She was unresponsive. She had nothing to hope
for; she might as well be dead. She looked at him. Then at Bernice.
She managed a strange little grin. Solomon asked her to sit down.
She obeyed. He asked her if she would like a drink. She shook her
head. He then looked at Gladys Walton and asked her if she would
like to sit down. She chose a straight-back-chair near Olive. He asked
her if she would like a drink. No, she did not drink she told him.
He turned back to Olive, who was still shaking her head, refusing
a drink. Solomon looked at Bernice. They were both uneasy. They
didn't know what to say. Olive was ill. She would have to be sent
home. Her doctor would have to be called.

Solomon Armsburg and Bernice had been having martinis when
Olive had arrived. They sat, slowly finishing their drinks. They
were waiting. Waiting for something to be said.

Suddenly Gladys stood up and said she thought she'd better take
Olive home and put her to bed.

The next morning, Olive could not get out of bed. She was too
weak to move. She seemed to have collapsed physically. Gladys

Walton called Solomon Armsburg. Doctors were called. Olive was taken back to the hospital. That night, Olive's heart failed. She died shortly after midnight.

Olive was alone when she died.

[MORRIS]

I wonder where I'll be in two weeks," Morris asked in a voice full of self-pity. He placed his glass down on the table in front of him and looked out vacantly from the sidewalk cafe of the Brevoort.

The heat pressed down in layers over Fifth Avenue. People ambled listlessly by. The sidewalk cafe was crowded. It was sheltered from the strong sun by an awning. Every table was occupied.

All around Morris and his friend, Norman Roth, people were talking. Morris glanced idly from table to table. His eyes stopped from time to time as he ravished some strange woman with his glance.

"Yes, I wonder where I'll be," Morris asked again.

"I wouldn't worry about it," Norman answered, his eyes following the figure of a passing female.

Morris lit a cigarette. A woman in red walked by. She looked fresh; she seemed to be untouched by the sweltering heat. Morris stared after her. God, to have a woman like that!

Neither of them spoke for a moment. Sweating waiters scuttled about. The conversation from nearby tables was ceaseless. Suddenly, the happy ring of a woman's laughter rose above the buzzing talk. Morris turned in the direction of the laughter. But he could not see her. He puffed on his cigarette.

Morris was about twenty-seven years old but he looked neither young nor old; he seemed ageless. Slightly under medium height, he was thin and sallow and wore a faint mustache. His face was weak and seemed to be fixed in an unhappy expression. Norman, stocky and healthy looking, yawned.

"This goddamned heat," he said.

"Yes, the damned heat," Morris said.

"It's even too hot for fornication," Norman commented.

"You'd have to be awfully hard up to want it in weather like this," Morris said glibly.

A tall attractive girl passed with a dog on a leash. They both stared after her.

"She could change my mind," Norman laughed.

"Yes, she could make a man forget the heat," Morris said, his voice still spiritless.

Norman signaled for the waiter. He ordered another gin and bitters for himself and a beer for Morris. Morris, slumped in the chair, nervously flung his cigarette out toward the curb. He lit another. His eyes wandered about the cafe. His expression was vacuous.

"I wonder where I'll be in two weeks," Morris asked himself aloud once more.

Norman didn't hear him. He was looking at a blonde a few tables away. Morris turned to see what had caught his friend's interest. Her beauty and animation had caught the eyes of many of the men. Morris lowered his eyes to her legs under the table. They were beautiful. She was the kind of girl men dreamed of. The man who possessed her would be the envy of all his friends. Morris turned wistfully back to his beer and took a sip.

"I don't like going to a new place," he said. "I always feel nervous about it. It isn't just being lonesome, it's worse than that."

"I don't understand your feelings about this trip," Norman said.

"Of course you don't, Norman. You're married. You're happy. If you were going on a trip like this, Helen would be going with you."

"How do you know I'm happy?"

Morris' face became alive with interest. He leaned forward eagerly.

"Well aren't you?"

"Who can be happy in times like these?"

Morris was disappointed.

"At least you're personally happy."

"Personal happiness doesn't mean much in these times," Norman said.

"I hate to be lonesome," Morris said, slumping down in his chair.

"Hell, Morris, you're young—younger than I am."

"I'm old enough to know how I feel."

"And you're unattached."

"Who wants to be unattached?"

"You should. I had two really lousy marriages before I met Helen."

"But you've got the right one now. And you make money from your writing. You don't have to take jobs like teaching or lecturing to make a living."

"That's true but I still wouldn't be worrying if I were in your position," Norman said, his eyes again moving in the direction of the animated blonde.

"I'm not worrying."

"Hell, why should you? You've got a good job, educational director of World Loans Incorporated. That's certainly better than teaching at a jerky little college upstate. You'll have a chance to travel. Man, you're going to see Russia. What the hell are you complaining about?"

"I'm not complaining. I guess I don't know what I want."

"You're lucky. After all, you're free. And you're doing something, too. You're taking people to the Soviet Union and giving them a chance to see how decent life can be instead of the stinking mess we have here in capitalist America. Christ, remember how you used to feel when you were teaching political science."

Morris said nothing.

"Well, I remember," Norman went on. "And I remember the way you were treated. You were the only Jew in the whole department and you were surrounded by reactionaries. And now you're going to Russia. Hell, man, you ought to be dancing in the streets."

"I guess so, Norman. I suppose it's the heat that has put me in the dumps."

Morris took another sip of his beer and looked around.

"I'm just lonesome. I don't like to travel alone."

"It's summer. You'll probably meet some beauties on the boat. And then there are the Russian girls. Christ, I envy you."

"Why don't you come along?"

"I would if I didn't have to go to Hollywood."

"I received my notice to travel in a week. I don't like getting such short notice."

Norman didn't comment. He finished his drink and looked at his watch.

"I have to shove along now. Cheer up, Morris, it's a hundred in the shade; you can sit here and relax. I'll see you for dinner tomorrow night, okay?"

"Sure."

Norman left money on the table for the bill and walked off. Morris sat glumly, staring at nothing.

Morris always griped. He blamed conditions in the world for his own depressed moods. He was never satisfied. In his first year as a political science instructor, he had managed to make himself the most unpopular man on the small faculty.

He had become a fellow traveler but he frequently had qualms because of this. He wanted to be more than just a fellow traveler. He wanted to be famous, to be respected, and to respect himself. His life seemed dull and dreary to him. But fellow traveling did help to fill the gap between what he wanted and what he had.

Most of the time, Morris believed that he was struggling to better the world. Society had made him pay a price. He hated it and he would help to destroy that society.

He had been offered his job through the efforts of a friend who was a member of the Party. The Party was always helping him and advising him. He sometimes fretted because of this—he had few decisions to make on his own. But at the same time, he was respected. He was invited to parties and given to understand that he was an insider. He earned more money now than he had teaching; and he wanted to see the world, despite his anxiety about traveling.

But there was Sylvia. She had been a student of his and had been active in the Communist Youth movement. She was a simple and unimaginative girl. Serious, loyal, and devoted, she gave most of her free time to Party work. She sold papers on streetcorners, got herself arrested for picketing, handed out leaflets, and attended meetings regularly. At first, he had admired her as a loyal and energetic rank-and-filer.

But now, he went to parties where the Party leaders, editors, and successful literary men who were close to the Party were all to be met. He had met well-known writers like Norman. He had changed his mind about Sylvia. She wasn't ugly but she didn't look glamorous or sexy. When she had been his student, she had seemed bright, alert, almost pretty. She had approached him to speak at the local Karl Marx club. After some hesitation, he had agreed to do so. Their affair had started soon after this. At first, he had been afraid. She might get him into trouble. But Sylvia had been honest and direct. She had placed no responsibility on him. A comrade, she had explained, did not treat sex as a means of property exploitation. For a short time, the affair had flattered his vanity.

But Morris soon found himself dissatisfied with her. At times, he appreciated her simple comradeliness and her naturalness about sex. Nonetheless, he did not get the satisfaction he wanted in a relationship with a woman. At odd moments, he would look at her with disappointment, measuring her against the women he met at parties or saw on the streets. At times he would experience physical revulsion at the sight of the hair under her arms. And besides, Sylvia was Jewish, and although he would never admit this to anyone, and could scarcely face the fact in his own mind, Morris knew that he wanted a Gentile girl.

In his fantasy life, he conquered and dominated women. Mixed in with these dreams of domination, there was a need to be conquered. He was a man with a deeply wounded vanity; and sex was a possible means of healing this wound.

Sylvia had fallen in love with him, and he resented this. His life had become organized around her. Their mutual friends thought of them as a couple in love; a practically married couple. At times, he spoke of themselves and of their relationship, declaring that they were not sweethearts but comrades, comrades whose love was untainted by bourgeois sentimentality about love. But this was not what he wanted.

Morris wanted to break off with her; and he didn't want to. He needed a mistress, one who was as much a mother as she was a sweetheart. He relied on Sylvia more and more; and he resented her because he needed her.

After he began to live a more interesting social life, Morris had become ashamed of Sylvia. The wives and sweethearts of the writers and intellectuals he met seemed to be more intelligent, more beautiful, and more attractive than Sylvia. They dressed better than she did. And they used perfume. They were mysteriously feminine. If he could sleep with one of them, he was certain that the experience would be more gratifying than it was when he slept with Sylvia.

He became more irritable with her. And silently, he became more critical of her body. But he was guiltily aware of her loyalty and devotion. He wouldn't be able to face himself, he feared, if he were to suddenly break off with her.

And yet there was no mystery about Sylvia. Long since, he had come to know her so well that he could find nothing surprising, nothing adventurous in anything they did together. Her body was known to him. At times, his main interest in it was in finding flaws —discovering that her skin was not soft, that her hips were too large, her thighs too big, her breasts out of proportion, her backbone too prominent.

In contrast, the other women he met seemed alluring and desirable. He wanted to see them naked, to possess them. He wanted new flesh. Morris would gaze lecherously at them. He would make oblique and suggestive statements, but of a kind that could not be taken as open invitations. He was afraid that if he tried to seduce one of them and failed, he would seem ridiculous.

He became particularly interested in the mistress of a new friend of his, Coleman Frank. Like Morris, Frank was a newcomer within the Party orbit. He had been one of the many young men of the 1920's who had set out to write the great American novel and become the American Dostoevski. His first novel, autobiographical in character, had been promising. But after it, he found himself unable to write. Finally, he had written a second novel. This had received a bad press and had a bad sale. But on the strength of the reputation he had gained with his first novel, he had been offered a Hollywood contract. Gradually, he had worked himself up to become a top-notch Hollywood scenarist. He assumed all the airs of a great artist. Thanks to his financial contributions to the movement, he was

treated with respect by the comrades. He often acted like a con-
spiratorial revolutionist.

His mistress was a beautiful red-haired woman who had played
several minor roles in pictures but who had retired. Morris believed
that her friendliness to him was genuine. He was flattered to be
asked frequently to Frank's home in the Village. There he met other
Party people—writers, actors, and Hollywood directors with social
conscience. He was treated as a good friend, and a poor relation.
Whenever he took Sylvia there, he would compare her with Frank's
mistress. Sylvia's manners seemed gauche. Her voice was too harsh;
her movements awkward. She dressed drably. The Revolution did
not propose that women should be unattractive. Socialism would
make women equal—and more beautiful. Sylvia's lack of concern
about her appearance expressed her infantile leftism.

M orris ordered another beer. He sat alone, hot and sad, thinking of himself and of Sylvia. He was going to Russia. He stared out
to the street. A Fifth Avenue bus rumbled by.

Suddenly, he heard his name called out.

"Morris."

He turned. Coleman and Jane were walking toward his table. He
was delighted to see them.

They sat down and ordered a drink. They were both rather quiet.
Conversation was sporadic.

"This place makes me think of Paris," Jane said.

"Let's go there this summer," Coleman said.

"Oh, let's. I'm dying to see Paris again."

"I think I could work better there."

Morris was jealous. He had never been to Paris. Would he ever
get there? This was only one of the many things he had missed in
life. He had never had a woman like Jane, either. She was so chic,
so lovely. He would never conquer the heart of such a woman. He
tried to visualize her naked.

The waiter brought two drinks to the table for Coleman and Jane. Morris switched from beer to scotch and soda.

Coleman started talking of Hollywood. Another world of glamor of which he had been deprived. He grew more sullen.

"You don't look cheerful today, Morris," Jane said.

He forced a smile.

"Oh, it's nothing. I was thinking of how rotten the world is."

"Of course it is. But it's spring and you're going to Russia," Coleman said.

Some people walked in who knew Coleman. They joined them. In rearranging the chairs, Morris crowded himself next to Jane. His right leg touched her knee, inflaming him. He glanced at her but she was looking in the other direction. She didn't withdraw her knee. Perhaps? He began to hope. He looked at Coleman. Coleman was a big and awkward man with an ugly angular face, an uncouth voice, and a slouching walk. How could a woman as lovely as Jane want to be with such a man?

Morris ordered another drink to cheer himself up. He schemed as to how he could keep the party going. If so, they might decide to eat together. He would suggest a place where there was dancing. He could dance with Jane and he would be able to hold her body tightly to him.

He kept drinking. He became a little more bold and pressed his leg firmly against Jane's. He began to talk about love and freedom.

"I knew the scotch would pep Morris up," Coleman remarked.

Morris grinned. He was happy now. The mere contact of his leg with her body rendered her mysterious. To solve that mystery— how ecstatic it would be!

Sylvia walked by and saw them. She joined them. She was crushed in between Morris and Jane. It was just his luck. He looked at her sourly. When she asked him how he felt, he answered her in a curt monosyllable. He sat beside her, hating her.

Soon after this, the party broke up. It was nearly seven. All these people were leaving for pleasant dinners, for activities which interested them. He? He was alone with Sylvia.

"What's the matter with you today, Morris?" she asked.

"Nothing. Why?"

"You seem in an unpleasant mood."

"Do I always have to grin like an idiot? Besides, who can be happy in this society?"

"But, darling, it's spring, and you're going away on such a wonderful trip."

"Yes," he growled.

"You're troubled, Morris, what's on your mind?"

"Nothing. It's so hot; I don't feel good."

"Well let's go home. I'll fix you dinner. Do you have anything there I can fix?"

"I don't know. Come on, let's go see."

He took her arm and grimly marched her to his apartment. There, he brutally tore her clothes off and possessed her in a cold and calculating way, as if by doing so, he were punishing her.

Then, he lay in bed, spent, disgusted with himself, and thinking that if only she had not come along, he might have managed something with Jane.

"Darling, you seem so strange," she said, lying beside him.

"Get over here again," he ordered.

She obeyed.

He tried to further humiliate her in sex. Finally, he was utterly exhausted. And he was disgusted with himself. He lay beside her, hating her.

She got out of bed, dressed, went out, and bought food in a delicatessen. When she returned, he was sleeping. She quietly prepared a meal and then awakened him with a soft kiss on the forehead. He got out of bed, put on a bathrobe, and sat down to eat. He had a headache from the whiskey he had drunk. Silently, he ate in boredom.

After eating, he took her to a movie and sat slouched down in the seat. He thought of Jane. Were she and Coleman in bed now?

He went home writhing in self-disgust. He went to sleep asking himself where he would be in two weeks, and wondering if anything would ever happen to change his life.

[BENJAMIN MANDLEBAUM]

Benjamin Mandlebaum arrived in Chicago when he was eighteen years old. He brought with him a few clothes, five dollars, and a folder filled with poems. He rented a cubicle for fifteen cents a night in a flophouse called The Deluxe on West Madison Avenue. The fact that it was dirty didn't bother him.

Benjamin Mandlebaum received recognition as a young poet. From the start, he assumed the airs of a great writer. He craved praise but he was so afraid of being laughed at that he adopted a pseudo Swiftian manner and insulted people.

Mandlebaum soon won recognition in Chicago.

Benjamin Mandlebaum's father had been a peddler. He died when Benjy was five. Benjy had only vague memories of him.

But he remembered his mother. She had been a squat, dark-haired woman who had never wanted children. But Herman Mandlebaum had insisted, what kind of home was it where there weren't children.

Benjy was born in Mobile, Alabama.

When Herman Mandlebaum died, he left less in effects than he had in memory. And Mrs. Mandlebaum blamed Benjy for her troubles. He was a burden; a thorn in her life. She screamed and cursed at him constantly. Benjy never complained. Even when she went out to eat alone and let him go to sleep hungry, he never said anything. He was scared, scared of what she could do.

Benjamin Mandlebaum was almost seven when he was put in an orphan asylum. His mother had threatened to do this many times. Yet when it happened, Benjy Mandlebaum was numb with terror.

For the first few weeks, he was on his best behavior. He answered questions, spoke when spoken to. His mother was only trying to scare him. As soon as she found out how good he could be, she would come get him. She wouldn't leave him here.

As the weeks passed, Benjy became silent. Then cautious. He was not being punished, he was being tested. It was a game his mother was playing on him. All he had to do was behave himself and not make any trouble. If he didn't disobey, didn't cry or scream, his mother would come get him.

Benjy began to believe that he remembered his mother telling him that she was going to play this game on him. She even explained the rules. Yes, he could remember her words exactly.

Each morning, he woke up telling himself that this might be the day the game would end. His mother would come to get him and she would be like other mothers. She would like him and sometimes be nice to him.

Benjy Mandlebaum believed this because he knew that he had no other chance of getting out and he hated the place. He was kicked, slapped, and punched; called a little Jew bastard, a kike.

The days were slow and hard. Occasionally he daydreamed about being home with his mother. In these dreams, she would tell him how much she missed him while he was in that awful place. His face would become blissful.

A slap would remind him where he was.

"O.K., you little Jew bastard. You think you're gonna stay in bed forever and let the other fellows do your work. Up with you."

By the end of his first month, Benjamin Mandlebaum knew that his mother was not coming. He had been abandoned.

Although the orphan kids fought among themselves, they were united against all adults, the ones who worked in the asylum, benefactors and benefactresses, Christians who were good to orphan kids, and the ones who had abandoned them.

Benjy Mandlebaum never became popular but in time, he did become less unpopular. Newcomers were new game and Benjy would join in tormenting them. He would feel a pity for the victim but he kept silent. He might be turned on by the pack if he showed this pity.

Benjy Mandlebaum did not forget his mother. She had dumped him here. For this he hated her.

Benjy was hurt more by his fantasy than by what his mother had actually done. In his fantasy, he and his mother were playing a game. He had behaved himself and gone by the rules but his mother had not come to get him. He hated her for not keeping the agreement that he imagined she had made with him.

Days were long for Benjy Mandlebaum. And the years became a collection of long days.

The orphanage changed from a strange to a familiar place. The familiarity was worse than the strangeness had been. Hope was lost.

Gradually, his memory of his mother grew dim and that of his father was almost lost. He didn't remember the details of her leaving him here but he knew that she had tricked him and that he would get even with her some day. He didn't know how, but he would get even.

Benjy Mandlebaum was not a stupid boy. Nor was he crazy. He was troubled and unhappy. He was unloved and could only pour his capacity for love upon himself. When he was mistreated, his feelings of love were affronted and his reaction was all the stronger. No wound of spirit could be slight to him.

He was growing. He was gradually getting bigger, and smaller kids kept coming into the place. They got the same treatment he had gotten. Whatever the new kid got, the new kid had to take. That was part of the code.

The older boys in the orphanage often talked about running away. Benjy Mandlebaum was no exception.

"Once I get out of here."

He liked the idea of being free. The orphanage was not as bad now as it was when he was a kid. He'd learned some of the ropes. And he'd learned how to insult his tormenters with sarcastic comments.

Various ministers visited the orphan asylum. Occasionally a rabbi or priest would come. Some of the clergymen would get the boys out to do various kinds of work around their churches and parsonages.

One of these was a Reverend Holcomb. He was in his late thirties but he looked much younger. He was thin. Soft in speech and in body. There was something prim about him. When he held services at the orphanage, he stressed purity. He always told the older boys that if they had any problems, any worries or difficulties, they could always come to him. They would find that he had an ear.

And whatever they said would be held in complete confidence. He wanted them to look upon him as a friend; he was not a holier-than-thou, even though, as a minister of God, he did try to be a little bit holy. Everybody should try, not only ministers of God. But to be holy was different from holier than thou. Jesus, the Son of our Lord God, had not been holier than thou and He had been the most holy of all.

There was something about the Reverend Holcomb that the boys didn't like. They were relieved when he left. Sometimes when he took a boy out to his parsonage to do some work, the boy would return silent. The other boys would ask him if he liked being on the outside. Was it exciting?

"It's all right, I guess."

"What happened?"

"Nothin'!"

The boys were quiet and observant. They caught on to things that happened.

And they caught on to the Reverend Holcomb.

Benjy Mandlebaum did not want to go to the Reverend Holcomb's; and yet there was a fascination with the idea. For one thing, he would be out of this place. He wished Saturday would hurry up and come.

He didn't like Reverend Holcomb. One of the other boys, a good fighter named Starky, had asked Benjy what he thought of him. Benjy had answered: "He's a Jesus Christ who will slap you on the wrist."

Starky had laughed.

"Wait till I tell the other kids what you said, that's a good one, Benjy."

Benjy valued this praise. He was glad he hadn't told Starky what he really thought of Reverend Holcomb. Honesty was the best policy only if you wanted to get into trouble. No one in the orphanage cared about honesty. The only thing they cared about was not getting caught. A kid had to say or do what was best for him. There was no need to talk about it.

Once, when Ben Harmon was suspected of stealing, he was ordered to see Mr. Highgate, who was superintendent of the place. Starky had warned him.

"Do you wanna get treated like a nigger?"

"No."

"Well then don't tell the truth to Highguts."

Ben Harmon knew that Starky was right. He didn't tell the truth. He got whacked and was made to do extra work in the kitchen during play time.

"You'd have got worse if you'd told," Starky told him.

And Ben Harmon guessed that Starky was right. That's why the kids always laughed about Reverend Holcomb's sermons. He was always saying things like: "If you lie, you sin against God, our Father." "When you lie, you transgress the law of God."

Benjy Mandlebaum thought that Reverend Holcomb's sermons were silly. And he guessed that he would be hearing a lot of the same things when he went over to the parsonage on Saturday, but still, he was curious.

By the time Saturday came, Benjy was afraid. He tried to get off going by pretending to be sick. But his pretense didn't work. A little after nine o'clock, Reverend Holcomb came to get him. Robby Langford was supposed to go, too, but Robby really was sick with a sore throat and was excused from going. Benjy Mandlebaum was enraged. He didn't think that Robby was sick, no more than he was.

R everend Holcomb was married. If the Reverend hadn't married Delilah Stone, there was good reason to believe that Delilah would never have been married. It was difficult to understand why he had married her. He himself often wondered. As time passed, he tried to think that he had married her out of pity; not knowing that he, a pitiless man, could only pity after the fact.

He married Delilah Stone out of inexperience.

He had been young, a newly ordained minister. He lived by the morals that were accepted tenets of the faith he preached. The Reverend Holcomb was sincere; he tried to be good. But he was beset with temptations. And he was lonely. He was separated from people by virtue.

He ought to have a wife. This was not an original idea; it had been suggested to him regularly. He would always smile. But the idea of having a wife depressed him. He feared that he was depraved. He had committed Onan's sin many times; too many times. Even once was too many. He was ashamed. He was on his way to total depravity.

—Lord Jesus Christ, Lamb of God, I have been more bestial than the beasts of the field. I am an unworthy minister of Thy gospel.

The young Reverend Holcomb had been sitting before an old roll-top desk where he was trying to write a sermon. He could hear the outdoor sounds. It was a lazy spring afternoon. The air was fragrant and sensuous. He became drowsy. He languidly put his pen into the inkwell. He heard a bee outside the window. A bumbling buzzing bumble bee. That would be a good line for boys who stutter. A bumbling buzzing bumble bee. Thank the Lord, he was not a stutterer.

—No!

This time he meant it.

—No!

This time it was a slower and weaker no.

He didn't want to, he really didn't want to. He would try to concentrate on what he was writing. That way he wouldn't think about the feeling he could get if he . . .

In an outbreak of desperation, the young Reverend Holcomb frenziedly committed the sin of Onan once more.

Afterward, a feeling of guilt swept over him. He could not undo what he had done. If only he had not succumbed. His hands were unclean. He had defiled his hands; he had defiled himself. He was a vessel of God and he had defiled God's vessel.

He sat slumped in a chair, his trousers unbuttoned, exposing his limp organ. He looked down at himself. He should get down on bent knees and pray. He should pray for forgiveness. And for strength.

As the weeks went by and the young Reverend Holcomb succumbed to temptation again and again, he became terrified lest his secret sin be discovered. He had to cure himself. Maybe he could by marriage. But women were a mystery to him; he was afraid of them. He always acted stiff and formal around them; he didn't know how to be otherwise.

The young Reverend Holcomb made his decision. He would get married.

But how does one go about finding a wife? There were not many eligible girls in the small community. Pickings were few. And the young Reverend Holcomb was a poor prospect as a provider. God paid him no wages; and His children did not pay much more. He was a humble minister of God, shepherding some of God's poor.

However, all things are relative, even undernourishment. And many of the young Reverend Holcomb's sheep had far less to eat than their shepherd. If not a catch, neither was the young Reverend Holcomb a miss. He was able to feed himself.

The young Reverend Holcomb's decision to marry was an urgent one. Every day, he was on the lookout for one who might become Mrs. Holcomb.

Every day, he believed he would meet her.

Every day, he resolved to desist from his shameful sin.

Every day, he looked. He would soon be married. He knew this. God would help him find a Mrs. Holcomb. And as soon as he was married, he would cease his sinful habit. And since he would not be committing this sin any more once he was married, and since he did not have a wife now to keep him from thus sinning, he . . . no, that was not right. He was not thinking clearly. The act of Onan was a sin. The young Reverend Holcomb was confused. His sense of sin strengthened his determination to get married.

He kept resolving and reresolving. He promised God anew. But flesh is not promise keeping.

Again and again, he would repeat the sin of Onan.

It was in desperation, filled with a strong and guilt-stained unworthiness, that the young Reverend Holcomb married one of God's lowliest and poorest creatures, Delilah Stone.

Delilah Stone looked like a scarecrow. She was skinny and bony; she even had three front teeth missing. Her family lived just outside town.

The marriage took place in the little wooden church where Reverend Holcomb preached to his flock. The church was almost full. Delilah's relatives accounted for the almost full church. Not too many of the young Reverend Holcomb's sheep were there. Delilah Stone had a reputation. The sheep of Holcomb's flock were outraged.

The Reverend Seth Tilson married them. The Reverend Tilson had had carnal knowledge of Delilah Stone about four times. But the Reverend Tilson had no great wrenches of conscience about such doings. God had given him an itch for poontang. That's why he had it, as often as he could.

The Reverend Tilson maintained a pious expression on his somewhat ravaged face as he performed the ceremony. He was a little condescending to the young Reverend Holcomb.

The young Reverend Holcomb was in a daze. He knew what was happening but it was like a dream.

After the wedding and the party, the young Reverend Holcomb and his wife had gone off on a honeymoon for a week in Jackson, Mississippi.

Although they had stayed at the party for just a short while, Delilah's family were all almost drunk before the bride and groom left. Delilah herself had had a few drinks and their effect was obvious. Normally, she wasn't one for talking. She didn't have much to talk about.

—Delilah may not be teched but she's slow.

This is what many of the people in the community said about her. And nobody denied it.

But after a few drinks, after her wedding, Delilah talked. And the way she talked. In front of a minister of the gospel. Even though he was her husband, that was no excuse.

The young Reverend Holcomb's face was flushed. It stayed flushed later when they were on the train. Delilah almost crawled on top of him right in front of the other passengers. And him wearing his collar. Delilah pawed him all the way to Jackson. He was mortified. He turned a deeper shade of pink when he heard some loud guffawing from the seat across the aisle.

—There's a preacher who likes his poontang.

He didn't know what "poontang" meant but he could give a good guess. He reminded himself that his work was God's work. He was not without sin but he was a minister. And now he was a husband, too. As a husband, he had the right. And Delilah had the obligation to obey, and do as he commanded. But the young Reverend Holcomb hesitated to take his rights. He did not know what would happen.

That night, as soon as they were alone, Delilah began to slobber kisses on him and paw him. They went to bed.

"Put the Lord in me," she screamed.

And: "Put the Lord in me again!"

There was nothing else to do with Delilah.

The young Reverend Holcomb was released from the clutches of the sin of Onan; he was released from his guilt.

When the young Reverend Holcomb returned from Jackson, Mississippi, with his wife, he went about the Lord's work just as he'd done before he took Delilah to have and to hold.

Things were different. They seemed different. But only a week had gone by since he had gone away. Things couldn't be as different as he felt them to be. Neither could the people be so different. But there was a difference. The glory of the Lord seemed to have vanished from all that was around him, from the sheep of his flock, from himself, and from life. What was life without the glory of the Lord? He had married Delilah so that he could have some pleasure without sinning. He was no better off than he had been. Waves of self-disgust went through him.

Marriage was blessed in heaven. It was the means of gaining happiness on earth. But marriage to Delilah Stone was not giving him much happiness.

And there were members of his flock who did not seem to think much of his marriage. He was the butt of many jokes, most of them coarse. He flushed when he heard these behind his back; the young Reverend Holcomb was laughed at. Many of the men who laughed had had Delilah. The young Reverend Holcomb knew that Delilah had done her share of sinning but he didn't know how much.

Time passed. The young Reverend Holcomb was now The Reverend Holcomb. His sermons were better. His flock came to think of him as a right smart parson. Yessirree, the parson had some good ideas and he had a good way of tellin' 'em.

This had happened by grace of the fact that a salesman passing through the town had seen Delilah, caught her eye, and followed her until they reached a cotton field. There, after giving her a few smacks from a bottle, she had given him a few whacks in return.

Later, when he found out that she was a parson's wife, he was worried. He didn't want to get on the wrong side of a minister of God.

That's when he got the idea of giving the Reverend Holcomb a copy of Elbert Hubbard's Scrapbook. His wife's brother had given him the book, hoping that it would be a means of improvement in his life.

Reverend Holcomb accepted the book and thanked him for the gift. He wondered at the time if the salesman had gotten Delilah in some field somewhere and was feeling guilty about it. But he guessed not; the salesman hadn't been in town long enough.

Reverend Holcomb thanked him for the book and invited him, if he was ever in town on a Sunday, to come in for services. The salesman said that yes, he certainly would, but that he wouldn't be able to on this trip. In fact, he was on his way out of town now. With this, he got ready to leave. He had not seen Delilah but he had heard movements from the back of the house. He gathered that it must be her back there; he was glad she hadn't come out front.

The Reverend Holcomb had long since impressed on Delilah that she was not to appear in the front of the house unless he told her so. She hadn't objected; this way she could sneak out the back way. She did, often.

She did that day, and the salesman got one more whack at her in the backyard of the parsonage.

In the house, the Reverend Holcomb glanced at the book and then put it aside.

A few days after, when he was trying to think about a sermon for the coming Sunday morning, he picked up the book and started looking through it. It was full of good things, things he could use. He took quotations from here and there.

—The preacher's a smart 'un, he is.

—He's a deep 'un all right.

—He's a lot smarter 'n he looks.

Talk about the preacher being smart began to supplant the talk about his marriage to Delilah. It was a relief to talk about how smart the preacher was instead of talking about his wife being a scarlet woman. Delilah did what a scarlet woman does but it was hard to think of her as a scarlet woman. She was too skinny, too homely, and she had been fornicating in the cotton fields for years.

This was the beginning of the Reverend Holcomb's rising reputation. He started using quotations from Elbert Hubbard's Scrapbook in all his sermons.

His reputation as a smart preacher grew.

Delilah, who had seemed such a drawback, was the cause of his advancement.

Church attendance increased and consequently, there was a rise in the collections. The increase in the coffers came to the attention of Bishop Merriweather.

The Bishop had officiated when the Reverend Holcomb was ordained but for the life of him, he couldn't place the young fellow. Still, there must be something worthy about him, something that reached the congregation. Bishop Merriweather decided to keep an eye on this fellow.

And he did. He grew convinced that this Reverend Holcomb was just the man to take over the congregation at Lindley. The coffers at Lindley used to be filled every Sunday, but something had happened to the Reverend Foote—the coffers told the Bishop this much.

The Reverend Holcomb received orders to go to Lindley, Mississippi.

The Reverend Holcomb decided that he would go on ahead and let Delilah follow later, the next day. It was important to make a good first impression.

He was right. He was liked in Lindley.

The deacons thought that the new preacher seemed cheerful. He had a nice smile, a real nice smile.

The Reverend Holcomb had not calculated to make himself what others thought he should be. He had not planned to acquire gestures and mannerisms that usurped the place of character traits.

His father had been a poor farmer, his mother not much better than Delilah. He'd gone hungry as a boy. His father was mean because of poverty and overwork. Whenever he could, he had gotten drunk on corn whiskey and beaten him and his mother. He beat all his children.

The Reverend Holcomb, as a boy, lived close to a level of subsistence. But if he behaved at Sunday School, the preacher praised him. If he ran errands promptly, was honest, and pleased others, he was rewarded. He had learned his lessons of conduct, of escaping from a life such as that of his parents, by learning to be as others wanted him to be.

It was the preacher and the rich members of the church who had decided that a boy as good as he was should be educated for the ministry. This was how he had become a minister of the gospel.

In Lindley, Mississippi, the Reverend Holcomb became one of God's fixtures. He still confined Delilah to the back of the house. Now, she and six children lived back there. The kids might have been his, he thought, but he couldn't prove it. He had had carnal usage of Delilah; he was not an uncarnal man. But his carnal eagerness always led to disgust. And he was a lazy man. To have full carnal satisfaction of a woman required effort, strenuous effort.

He had learned this at a conference with fellow shepherds which was held in Atlanta, Georgia. At the conference, he was led into a carnal congress with a sister of the faith. The sister of the faith had carried on something wild. She got him as naked as Adam, and she was as naked as Mother Eve. She said that she knew it was wrong, that she was sinning, but that she had to do it. She carried on like a wild woman. She moaned and cried. She used words the Reverend Holcomb had never heard. She kept begging him for more, she wanted more. She begged him to do it again, she wanted him to do everything to her, everything that he could. It was a wonder she hadn't been turned into a pillar of salt right then and there in that hotel room in Atlanta.

"Preacher, preach it to me again."

He remembered her saying that. And saying: "Ooooh, carnal knowledge is short for fucking. Ooooh."

His back ached but she begged him for more. Finally: "I just can't, Sister Eliza."

That was her name. Eliza Goodwill.

After that afternoon, he couldn't go to any more meetings. He fell asleep and slept for hours. When he woke up, he was still exhausted. He was due at a meeting but he decided not to go. He couldn't. He closed his eyes again. Tired as he was, he couldn't sleep. Guilt kept him awake. He had never in his whole life sinned as he had, right here in this room, with Sister Eliza. He wished he could sleep so he could forget. He could not stand it. He got out of bed and dressed quickly. He arrived at the meeting late. His entrance was conspicuous; so was his haggard face. He was excused from speaking at the request of Bishop Merriweather. It was plain to see that the Reverend Holcomb was overworked, the Bishop thought.

Sister Eliza was sitting far back in the audience in a side aisle. She smiled secretly.

Going out, Reverend Holcomb tried to avoid her. But he failed. He was about to pass through the open door of the room in which the meeting had been held when Sister Eliza Goodwill, without intention, came face to face with him. They almost collided.

"Howdy, Reverend Hallelujah," she said, and passed on by.

He was saved again. He could go back to his room and sleep. He went back to his room, pulled down the shade, and removed his clothes. He flung himself across the bed. He was tired, dead tired.

In a few minutes he was sleeping soundly.

When Reverend Holcomb returned to Lindley from the Conference in Atlanta, he seemed restrained. He could not shake off the memory of his sin with Sister Eliza Goodwill.

He was still ashamed and silent on the second day.

On the third day, he seemed pretty much the same.

The change was beginning. There were moments when he was not so silent.

He had sinned and neither Atlanta, Georgia, nor Lindley, Mississippi, had been turned into Sodom or Gomorrah. He had not been struck down by a bolt of lightning. He had not been punished and so far as he knew, neither had Sister Eliza.

Another day passed.

And another day.

The burden of his sin lightened with each day.

He began to smile again.

It was at this time that the Reverend Holcomb decided not to cohabit with his wife any more. She was his lawfully wedded wife; it wasn't a sin, but it was the same as a sin in his mind. He would refrain from it. Staying away from Delilah was like walking in the light of the Lord. He beamed with self-approval. He was walking in the light of the Lord. He smiled more often.

The people of Lindley noticed this. It was a right good sight to see, the happy beaming face of their parson. They had to hand it to him; he was by far the best parson Lindley ever had.

And the cotton crop was the best in many a year. Many members of his flock were convinced that the Reverend Holcomb had something to do with the good crop.

The Reverend Holcomb resumed the sin of his youth. He discovered that Onan's sin was more to be desired than the virtue of having Delilah. The guilt was not as long lasting; he could bear it more easily.

As for Delilah, she decided that if the parson didn't want to put the Lord in her any more, there were more than enough others ready to put the Devil in her and the Devil and the Lord felt pretty much the same way in her. She had enough to eat, she had a roof over her head. She had nothing to complain about. When her folks came to Lindley to see her, she had food to give them.

"Delilah, you never ate so good before you and the parson got married." Her relatives would say this to her.

"You never ate so good neither," she would answer.

By the time he reached his late thirties, the Reverend Holcomb was an important figure in Lindley, Mississippi. He was always called upon to do good for his fellow man; and he did, especially powerful and important fellow men.

At about this time, the Reverend Holcomb became interested in the orphan asylum right outside the town limits.

On his first visit to the orphanage, there was a strain between him and the boys.

A day or so after this visit, he began to think of them, the way they had looked. He wished they had liked him. On his next visit he would try to impress upon them that they had a friend in him. He would do something for them, he didn't know what, but it would be something. His second visit was very much like his first visit. The boys were polite but silent.

Mr. Highgate welcomed him. It would sound good in his report to say that the Reverend Holcomb had paid a second visit to the institution. He could add a flourish about the beneficial effects of these visits.

The Reverend Holcomb's visits continued. They were soon put on a scheduled basis.

He found himself looking forward to these visits. There was something winning about the boys. They were like puppies that you wanted to pat on the head. He liked to watch them; he wished he could get closer to them. But so far he hadn't been able to.

Mr. Highgate told him that he was having a good influence on them. The Reverend Holcomb said that it was rewarding work.

Word soon spread about the good work that the Reverend Holcomb was doing. Mr. Highgate saw to this; and he saw to it that his own role was not overlooked.

"They don't come no finer than Mr. Highgate."

Whenever someone made such a remark in his presence, Mr. Highgate would say: "I do the best I can."

It was Mr. Highgate who first suggested that the Reverend Holcomb take a couple of boys home to visit on weekends, to give them a taste of what a Christian home was like.

The Reverend Holcomb readily agreed to this. He was getting to like the boys.

The boys could perform chores around the house. They would cut the grass. Or paint a door. Put a barrel in the shed. The Reverend Holcomb always had some chore to assign to the boys.

After the boys had been visiting for several Saturdays, Reverend Holcomb began to spend more time with them. He talked to them more. He would take them down to Lindley Creek and let them swim. Just to be sure that nothing happened, no drowning or anything, he would sit and watch them swim and splash around. Then,

the Reverend Holcomb decided that he would swim with them.
He ordered a one-piece bathing suit through the mail.
Reverend Holcomb could not swim. He was afraid of the water.
The kids laughed at him behind his back.

He was sincerely trying to help these boys by bringing a little
happiness into their pitiful lives. He liked hearing them laugh and
talk but the boys gave him no more than cold-hearted obedience.
When he realized this, the Reverend Holcomb tried all the more
earnestly to prove his interest in them, but the boys remained dis-
trustful. They didn't like him; he was a minister, a friend of Mr.
Highgate's, an adult from the outside world. The boys had other
reasons for not liking him. They didn't like the way they felt if
he happened to touch one of them or brush up against them.

"He makes me want to puke," Starky had said.

They didn't like the way he looked at them sometimes.

They didn't like the way he talked to them.

The boys sensed that there was something about him that was
a threat. But it was Starky who finally spat it out: "He's too dumb
to know what he wants to do to us."

Benjy Mandlebaum had heard all this. That was one reason
why he was afraid to go to the Reverend Holcomb's house.

When the Reverend Holcomb learned that Robby Langford was
sick and couldn't come, he asked Mr. Highgate if there were some
other boy who would want to come. This made Benjy Mandlebaum
feel better; at least he wouldn't be alone.

When they reached the Reverend Holcomb's house, Benjy Mandlebaum disappeared. The Reverend Holcomb called him but there
was no answer. He walked down to the creek and back. He began
to worry. He kept calling out. Still looking, he happened to walk
by the back of his house. From an open window, he heard his wife,
Delilah: "You can put the Devil in me again, as many times as you
want, but don't pinch me. I don't like bein' pinched."

Benjy Mandlebaum became the hero of the orphan asylum.
He had fucked the minister's wife. He lorded it over the others.
Whenever the boys asked him what it felt like, he told them to go
find out for themselves.

"You boys can go jack off. I did what a man does. I put it into
the minister's wife," he'd say, sneering.

He was paying them back for all the lousy tricks, the busts in
the nose, the cracks on the jaw.

"That Jew's got a swelled head. Just because he fucked Reverend
Holcomb's wife, he thinks he craps gold," Starky said to his gang.

Buddy Blaine told Mr. Highgate about what Benjy Mandlebaum
had done. Buddy, a stupid-looking tow-haired boy whose mother
and father were in jail, was Mr. Highgate's stool pigeon.

Mr. Highgate pretended to be angry. But when Buddy left the
room, he laughed. This was one of the funniest things that had
happened at the Lindley Orphan Asylum since he had come here
as superintendent. Of course he shouldn't allow the deed to go un-
punished; it would set a bad example, he'd have to crack down on
Mandlebaum.

Mr. Highgate sent for Benjy.

There was a mild rap on the door of his office.

"Come in," he barked.

Nothing happened.

"Come in," he repeated loudly.

"I'm comin'," Benjy Mandlebaum said.

"What did you say, Mandlebaum?"

"I said that I was coming in, sir."

"All right, I didn't hear the sir."

Mr. Highgate sat down. He let Benjy Mandlebaum remain standing.

"Mandlebaum!"

Mr. Highgate demanded that he "own up." Benjy played dumb;
he didn't know what to own up for.

"Don't stand there, Mandlebaum, and pretend you don't know
what I'm talking about."

"But sir, I don't know."

"All right, Mandlebaum, you've had your warning."

"But I don't know."

"This is your last chance. Own up, Mandlebaum."

Mr. Highgate didn't really care whether or not Benjy Mandlebaum admitted his guilt. He was going to punish him.

Benjy Mandlebaum got a whipping and was put in solitary confinement for a week.

When he got out, he ran away from the orphan asylum.

Only a casual effort was made to find him. He was not found.

Benjy Mandlebaum became a young tramp, a hobo. At first he was afraid that he would be caught and taken back. He wanted to put as much dust between him and Lindley, Mississippi, as he could.

Benjy Mandlebaum hadn't stayed in any one place long, not until he arrived in the Englewood Station in Chicago in 1912 when he was eighteen years old.

Benjy Mandlebaum woke up with the overhead light glaring down upon him. He was in a bathtub, fully clothed. For an instant, he was terrified. Then he remembered. He had been at a party here. Where was everybody? He heard no sounds. He was sopping wet. Who had put him in the tub?

Clumsily, Benjy got out. He stood, holding on to a towel rack. His clothes were heavy; they were soaked. He bent down and squeezed water from his trousers around one ankle. He reached his hand into his pocket. He pulled out his corncob pipe; it was sopping wet. So was his half-full pack of Tip Top Tobacco. He flung it on the floor.

—For Philistine molecules.

He staggered out of the bathroom. Glasses were on the table, on the floor, on bookshelves and on the mantlepiece. Ashtrays were spilling over with cigarette butts. Several books from a bookshelf were on the floor. A dirty handkerchief lay on the piano keys. The punch bowl, still half filled, was on the table. Benjy staggered over to it, picked up a dirty glass from the table and dipped it in. He took a big swallow, spilling some on his chin and down the front of his clothes. He guzzled the whole glass this way and dipped it back into the punch bowl for another drink.

Where had they all gone? If he could find them, he could tell them a thing or two. He, the American Verlaine, could tell them what they were. He took another swallow of punch.

He was alone; and he was drunk. He knew that he was drunk. He took another swallow. It had a bitter stale taste. He spat and poured the rest on the floor. He set the glass down on the table.

He wanted revenge, revenge on all the young nonentities who scorned him, the nonentities who would remain nonentities. He would go to find them. He would go out and away, out in the night to see the silver glory of the deceitful moon, the treasured celestial jewelry of the cold and laughing blue sky. Out and away to breathe the unfouled air of the unconquered inland lake.

Out and away!

[JOSHUA]

J osh will never get over May's death," Louise Waller said. All of us looked off moodily. We had all known May and her sudden death had been a stark reminder of our own impermanence.

"How long has she been dead now?" I asked.

"It's been a number of years," my wife, Phyllis, said.

"Oh—at least seven," Evelyn added.

"It's been six years," Louise stated.

"No," I intervened, "it was after the war had started; it was March, 1941."

"Yes, that's right, now I remember, March, 1941," Louise remarked.

"Joshua is all things to all men," Phyllis said.

Louise looked at her.

"I wouldn't say that, Phyllis. No, I don't think so. Not that I think I know him, I don't, even though Al and I were good friends of his for years."

"He is fascinating in his complexity," Evelyn commented.

"Tell me," I cut in, looking at Louise, "what does he do that makes you think he isn't getting over May's death?"

"Oh, for one thing, he walks the street all night. He'll walk with anyone he can find. And he's always complaining about aches and pains and endless symptoms. He has neuritis, and trouble with his stomach, and God knows what else. I think he wants to be ill."

"Guilt." Evelyn announced this with the authority of one who had been in analysis.

Joshua and I had been close for a time but still there had been a barrier. Friendship and intimacy had been more assumed than real. I had been to his house many times, and he to ours. Phyllis had known him longer than I. They had played together in a hit. In fact, gossip in the theatrical columns had insinuated a romance between them.

"Josh has changed," Louise said.

"I wonder," I mused aloud.

"He is not what he seems," Phyllis said.

"What do you mean by that?" asked Louise.

"What I said before, he's all things to all men," Phyllis repeated.

"Not really, not any more. He's harsh with people sometimes. Al and I both say it's too bad he wasn't that way years ago."

"Does he still play May's records?" asked Evelyn.

"Oh, yes, sometimes all night," Louise said.

"I should think that they would be worn out by now," Phyllis said.

"He's had new ones made. Al wanted to break them." Louise smiled.

"It sounds almost like necrophilia," Evelyn suggested.

I remembered when Phyllis had first spoken of Joshua to me. She had told me: "You want to like Joshua more than you can, more than he lets you like him."

"Joshua is one of the most fascinating men I know of to discuss; and I don't mean gossip about, I mean discuss," Phyllis said.

"He isn't a simple person. No, Josh isn't a simple man," Louise agreed, shaking her head.

"You and Al were very close to him, weren't you?" Phyllis asked.

"Oh, yes. Al adored him; you know Al. But he let Al down badly and now Al doesn't feel the same about him."

"How? How did he let Al down?"

"I'd rather not say, Phyllis. Al needed a friend; he relied on Josh and Josh let him down. It hurt Al a lot at the time but maybe it was good for him. Al is really much too trusting."

"Joshua will let anybody down in a pinch," I said.

"Oh, I don't think so," Louise defended him. "He's done many generous things for people, things that no one knows about."

"Perhaps, but that's a separate matter. Joshua always needs some support," I said.

"That's why he needed May," Evelyn said, nodding.

"But I think it's the way she died that bothers him so much," Louise said.

"I never knew what that story was. I read in the paper one day that she was dead. Since then I heard that she had had cancer and that she had been diagnosed incorrectly," Evelyn said.

"There's more to it than that," Louise said.

"What?" asked Phyllis.

"May was ill. She went to Dr. Kohlman," Louise began.

"Because he's a friend of Joshua's," added Phyllis.

"Any doctor can make a legitimate mistake," I said.

Louise went on.

"Kohlman didn't think that there was anything wrong with her. He thought her problem was psychosomatic. He sent her to another doctor, a Dr. Rudolph. Have you ever heard of him, Eddie?"

"No."

"He's a psychiatrist who can cure anything from bunions to melancholia. He told May that she was neurotic. Dr. Kohlman had said as much to her."

"And so she wasn't treated?" Phyllis asked.

"Didn't this Dr. Rudolph even bother to give her a physical examination?" I asked.

"Apparently not."

"That's ominous," I commented.

"Of course cancer can't always be detected. Kohlman had had X-rays taken. But you have to be able to read them. Actually, May should have been in a hospital where she could have a complete and careful checkup."

"What happened after that?" I asked.

"Joshua told her that her pains were all up here." Louise pointed to her head. "He told her that she had to put them out of her mind. He made plans to take her to Florida with him. And do you know what happened?"

"No, what?" asked Evelyn.

"The airlines didn't want to take her. By that time she weighed less than ninety pounds and she looked awful. Joshua had to sign a waiver or release or something. The airline people were afraid that she'd die on the plane. In order to fly down, she had to take them a letter signed by both Kohlman and Rudolph stating something to the effect that she was neurotic. They had recommended a doctor in Florida. Of course he told her that she was neurotic."

"What was his name?" asked Evelyn.

"Oh, I forget, but there she was, poor girl, on the beach exercising when she scarcely had the strength to stand up. When they flew her back here, they didn't think she would survive the flight. She was suffering intense pain but the doctors wouldn't give her anything; they still insisted that it was all in her head. It's no wonder, really, that Joshua broods about it."

"I wonder if there's more to it than that," I speculated.

"Like what?" asked Louise.

"I don't know."

To me, Joshua had first seemed to be a smooth human surface; but then, slowly, cracks in the form of contradictions had begun to show on that surface. When I met his coterie, I knew what Phyllis had meant when she said that I couldn't like Joshua as much as I wanted to. Coterie is the word that Phyllis and I used for Joshua's friends. You could rarely see him alone. He was surrounded by the coterie most of the time. To them, he was a great man. He would tell them about some of the famous people he knew on a first-name basis. He gave them a peripheral role in the Broadway-Hollywood literary world. He brought them together; it was his life that dictated their coming together. The coterie was composed of an odd assortment, but they all worshiped Joshua.

There was Phil Donlovan. Phil was just getting his break. The first thing that one noticed about him was his clothes. His suits were usually loudly striped and cut full. He always wore shiny belts and big ornate cuff links. His ties seemed to have been selected for their bizarre color combinations. Phil's voice was masculine and deep; he had been a sports commentator. Whenever I saw him, we talked about baseball. I wondered why he and Joshua were good friends; Joshua had no interest in sports and Phil had no interest that I knew of that could have struck a common chord with Joshua. Yet, they were close friends.

Joshua presented the same image to his coterie that he presented to the world at large. Central in that image was the conception of himself as that rare type—an actor with intelligence. He was supposed to be a student of logic and philosophy. On his bookshelves were the works of Santayana and one or two out-of-date treatises on logic. Joshua, logician and philosopher, was a significant and integral part of his public image. Joshua also appeared as a connoisseur, a man of taste and judgement. This admitted painters to the coterie. One of the painters was Bill Peterson. Phyllis and I were embarrassed when we met him. We had given a housewarming party. We had invited Joshua and May. Ours was a furnished apartment and several paintings that the landlady had picked up at auctions were hung on the wall. Among them were some paintings by Bill Peterson, a mediocre imitator of Cezanne.

At the party Phyllis mentioned that we were not responsible for the painting, that they had come with the furniture. One of those to whom she addressed this was Bill Peterson.

Joshua's coterie seemed to accept the fact that among them, only Joshua was great. I often heard some member of this group say: "Joshua is great, one of the great men of our time."

Joshua was at his weakest with them. He would sometimes talk of a subject to impress them. And he did not do this with others. At the same time, he was his most charming with them. He knew how they felt about him and he would relax. He would do imitations, give parlor characterizations, tell jokes, and quip. And Joshua could be very charming. He is a tall man with a bushy head of almost gray hair. His face is broad and somewhat coarse and yet there is something appealing about it. His features are irregular but somehow look attractive. His smile is warm and friendly, but the deep lines and the eyes suggest a man of experience, one to whom suffering is not alien.

Joshua is known as a fighting actor, one who is socially conscious. He fought the deadhead conservatives in Equity, demanding more democracy in the organization and better pay for young, bit-playing actors.

But there is another side to Joshua. And it is more difficult to evaluate. On several occasions, he and Phyllis found plays that they thought they could do together. On one occasion, they had a play

about Vienna which they both considered charming, a play which
would offer "a good night in the theatre." There were various meetings, efforts to interest potential backers. As this project went on,
Joshua's interest would wax and wane. They reached the point
where they had to work out a budget. Joshua wanted to keep it
down in order to get the play produced. Phyllis offered to cut her
own salary. Joshua set his own at seven hundred and fifty dollars
a week and would not budge. The salaries of all the other actors
had to be cut. Joshua was, at this same time, involved in a caucus
to get more money for actors playing bit parts. Finally, after the
budget had been drawn up and a prospective backer found, Joshua
announced that he could not go through with the plan. He had
heard that the prospective backer was a gangster. Joshua seemed
agitated. Phyllis and I did not know if he was merely suspicious
about the backer or if he had definite information. He kept describing it as gangster-tainted money.

"What difference does it make?" I asked.

"I couldn't, Eddie, I just couldn't," he said.

"It's only money. We're not dealing with morals here. We want
to get a play on. After all, any money that we'd get is tainted by
this social system."

"But I couldn't," he protested, smiling weakly.

Phyllis was agitated and I was afraid that she would denounce
him to his face and end all chances of getting the play on.

"Suppose he takes us for a ride?" Joshua asked.

"Why do you think he will? Why should he, for heaven's sakes?"
Phyllis demanded.

Joshua didn't know. But even if we weren't taken for a ride, we
would be responsible for bringing gangsters onto Broadway.

"They're all gangsters of one kind or another already," Phyllis
declared.

We urged, argued, and reasoned, but Joshua would not change
his mind. His manner was weak and helpless, apologetic at times;
but his position was stubborn.

It was after this that the friendship between us had cooled. But when I heard the news of May's death, I had gone to the services. And later, when her remains were taken from the vault and put into a grave, I went again. Joshua had seemed pleased, even grateful to see me.

As I came to realize that he was a weak man, I began to think of his acting differently. It seemed to me that his range was affected by his character. He could be charming and attractive but he could not play a role which required force. When he played Lear in *King Lear*, others expressed this opinion also. And his voice interfered with his playing the part. He could not act so much passion.

I thought of all this as the conversation went on about Joshua and May.

"Did he love her?" I asked.

Louise looked startled.

"Of course he did."

"In what sense?" I asked, speaking as much to myself as to the others.

"They were devoted," Phyllis said.

"You could see he adored her," Evelyn agreed.

I nodded; I was feeling my way through remembrances of Joshua.

"She knew she was going to die," Louise said.

"When? How long?"

"At the last, when she was taken off the plane after their trip to Florida. She was suffering intensely by then and she had said, 'I know I'm dying, can't you give me anything for the pain?' That's what troubles Joshua now, the fact that nothing was done for her."

"That can't be the only cause."

"Why, Eddie?"

"Joshua had accepted the diagnosis of each doctor, hadn't he?"

"But, Eddie, they're both reputable doctors."

"Perhaps, Louise, but had May been so neurotic, wouldn't Joshua have had some idea of it before it had gone so far?"

"I think Eddie's right," Evelyn said.

"It's almost as if he wanted to believe that she was neurotic,"

I went on.

This idea had never entered my head before but I suddenly felt as if I were close to a fresh insight.

"Maybe, maybe Joshua was projecting onto May. He had done this to such an extent that when the two doctors said that she was neurotic, he was prepared to accept the idea."

"Oh, Eddie, that sounds too complicated," Phyllis said.

"Well, there has to be some reason for him to be so guilt-ridden."

"Grief, perhaps." There was a sarcastic edge to Phyllis' voice.

"How separable are grief and guilt? And in this case, there is something more than meets the eye. Joshua has continued in much the same pattern for almost six years now."

No one spoke for a moment.

"Joshua acted somewhat as if he were May's son as well as her husband," I added.

"Not at first; there was some other man," Louise said.

"That's supposed to be a secret, isn't it?" asked Evelyn.

"I knew nothing of it," Phyllis said.

"Well," Evelyn said, "May was interested in some other man shortly after their marriage. She and Joshua almost broke up."

"Maybe he punished her after that," I suggested.

"Perhaps," Evelyn said.

"Well," Louise offered, "I know for a fact that she didn't do what she wanted to but what Joshua wanted her to do. It was because of him that she tried to sing for opera. She wanted to do lighter things but he insisted that she try to become an opera singer. He always dominated. His wishes were always the ones which ruled their lives."

"I wonder. I wonder if in a quiet way the real situation wasn't the opposite," Evelyn said.

"She was always doing things for him," Phyllis said.

"I was over there once. There were supposed to be four for dinner and a whole troop came in. Joshua said for them to sit down. He left it entirely up to May to see that they were fed. She ran out to the store. Joshua always assumed that May would take care of things," Evelyn said.

"He didn't seem to want to be alone with her, though. There was always his coterie. Their house was always filled with Joshua's admirers."

"That's not true, Eddie, there were times when he wouldn't let anyone in," Evelyn said.

"And he'd make her sing. She'd have to sing the same note over and over again until it satisfied him; and then they'd be perfectly happy," Louise said.

"How could she have been perfectly happy if she didn't want to be an opera singer?" I asked.

"Well, frankly, I never thought of that. Maybe she wasn't."

"And if so," I persisted, "it was only in the sense that she was sacrificing for him. If that was the case, she must have had needs corresponding to his."

"What needs?" Evelyn asked.

"I think one is clear. Joshua wanted a mother."

"Maybe, but his mother was an actress and an aunt took care of him. He talks about this aunt more than he does his mother," Evelyn said.

I looked at Louise. She was staring at me.

"Now that you mention it, Eddie, I always felt that there was something there. About his mother, that is."

"This is beginning to sound too schematic for me," Phyllis said.

"Once you break something like this down, the similarities are striking in their monotony," I explained.

"Anyway, Joshua seems changed now," Louise said.

"If it's true, it's terrible," said Phyllis.

"What do you mean?" Louise demanded.

"Simply this. If Joshua ever takes a tumble to himself, he'll never survive."

"Well, that's what I think is happening, he is taking a tumble to himself. You know Joshua was never short with people. He is now; he doesn't feel the same need he did to impress people," Louise said.

"I always thought Joshua had a kind of Christ idea of himself,"

Phyllis said.

I agreed, and added: "But it is a Christ image of a peculiar character. He wants to be Christ without preaching and without having any morality."

"What do you want him to do? Become a priest?" snapped Phyllis.

"I don't want him to become anything. I was merely saying that his Christ fixation seems real to me, but it is the idea of a drawing-room Christ, Christ on Broadway."

"That's not true, Eddie; look how he fights in Equity," Louise said.

"Yes, but he fights with support. He needs support. It gives him a feeling of security. And wasn't that pretty much what he got from May?"

"Yes," Louise admitted.

"Why is he still in the same mood as he was six years ago? Why doesn't he marry again? Why does he live with his two sisters?"

"He lived alone for a while but his two sisters took him to live with them," Louise said.

"Did he have to go?" I asked.

"Well," Louise paused. "No, but they do take care of him. I suppose you could say they mother him."

"I never could understand his attachment to his sisters," Phyllis said.

"Neither could I," Louise said, "they never felt that May was good enough for Joshua and they always had something to say about her. It does seem odd, doesn't it, if he's so guilt-ridden about May that he would move into their house now—they were never very nice to her."

"Has he shown any interest in another woman since May died?" I asked.

"May was his ideal," said Evelyn.

"But in what sense? She mothered him; she ran the house and saw that things were done for him. Isn't that so?" I asked.

"Yes. He reveals an archetype," said Evelyn. "And I know that

May wanted a child."

"Not at first. There was that abortion. But after that she wanted one badly but Joshua didn't. He said he wouldn't bring another Jew into this world. That's what he'd say, but I never believed that. I always felt that the reasons were more intimate; he would have had to change the basis of their relationship if there had been a child. A child would have been competition. I'm sure that this was the real reason. This is what disturbs him now. He all but says he wants to die. Al and I don't think that he's likely to get over it," Louise concluded.

"I still think you're all being schematic," Phyllis declared.

"Perhaps," I answered, "but it all fits. First of all, Joshua was a virgin until he married May. He was thirty-three years old. He's always had this close attachment to his sisters. It was obvious all along that May was somewhat of a mother to him. And then, Joshua is only brave when he has support. His own idealism is narrowed down when his own interest is involved. He rarely risks roles that are not comic or weak. He did in *Lear*, but that was the exception. Generally, Joshua is very fussy about the roles he'll play. The last time I saw him he was playing a Jewish waiter and was having a wonderful time on stage. The part called for skill and timing but not for much emotion. With all else, Josh is, you know, emotionally shallow."

"Why?" Phyllis asked.

"Because he's not mature. He's got too dependent a nature to have emotional depth. You know how he reacts to crises. He eats his heart out with unproductive grief."

"It adds up," Louise said.

"Well, maybe," Phyllis agreed.

Later, as we were leaving, Louise said: "Well, we certainly did take Joshua apart."

In a sense we had, but this had not been done in a personal way. There is more to be said than the conclusions we reached. While we had sat there and talked, Joshua was sitting in some other part of New York suffering. Our roughly made analysis was a psychologically structured one. And grief and suffering are more than a matter of psychological structure. On that night, as on other nights, Joshua may have tramped the streets alone, tearing his heart out, thinking of the girl who had loved him and had given him her life, the girl who is no more. Or he may have sat alone, listening to her records over and over again.

I thought of these things and the eagerness I had felt vanished. There was, in addition to the personal tragedy of Joshua, the untimely death of May.

I went to bed moody. I thought of Joshua. I remembered one Christmas when he had gone to a store and had bought twelve copies of one of my books and given them away as gifts. He had asked me to autograph these and then had sent them to Broadway-Hollywood famous people. I imagined him alone playing his records. Her voice preserved when all else was gone. Perhaps he was playing the one when she sang some light, happy song—as I had so often heard her sing.

[MARY ANNE READ]

ONE

Eddie Ryan looked around in the hotel dining room. It was almost empty. The Hotel Verve was expensive but not luxurious. Most of the tenants worked in the vicinity, either at the United Nations or in one of the advertising agencies in midtown Manhattan. Eddie looked at the clock. A little after ten. He should go back upstairs and try to do some work. He noticed Mr. Austin at a nearby table. What a pompous little man. After two massive coronaries, one would think that a man would begin to question some of his bourgeois values. He was not an unintelligent man but he seemed trapped in rigid boxes.

Eddie shook his head. No wonder he was having trouble with his writing. Shabby thinking. Why was he sentimentalizing about Dick Austin? He reached across the table to fold his New York *Times*. As he turned the page, he saw Loren Boorstein's name. It wasn't a long obituary, just a paragraph. It didn't say much. Loren had died after a brief illness. She was survived by a sister in New Jersey. It mentioned that she was the widow of George Boorstein, a well-known publishing figure of the Twenties.

Another of life's little ironies, Eddie thought. Last night he'd been rereading a novel by Mary Anne Read. George Boorstein had been the great love of her life. She had been dead for over thirty-five years. Eddie hadn't known her but he did know her work and it surprised him that a woman so vital should have fallen in love with George Boorstein. Not that George Boorstein wasn't a sweet man, he was. But he was also dull. Mary Anne Read had not lived long enough to become a public literary name but her two novels and her book of essays were still talked about occasionally.

Mary Anne Read was born in Richmond, Virginia, in the early 1900's. Her father was a lawyer, her mother of old Virginia stock. It had come to Eddie Ryan as a shock one day to realize that it had been as much a personal victory for Mary Anne Read to overcome her background and write as it had been for him. His problem had been that of a culturally impoverished environment. His grandmother couldn't read or write. Eddie could still remember how frightened she had been of his reading.

—All those books my grandson is reading; they'll be making an atheist of him. I'll have to be getting after the Devil. He'd better leave me son alone.

He still became angry when critics and English professors talked about his impoverished childhood. He'd been raised in his grandmother's home. In 1912, her apartment had cost his Uncle Al $125 a month. A cleaning woman came in once a week to do the heavy housework. And a laundress came in to do the laundry once a week. He had worn a clean shirt to school every day. He had never been hungry for food as a boy. But he had known another hunger—he had hungered to learn, and books were feared in his home.

Mary Anne Read's background was different, yet she had had to struggle, too. Her enemy was Southern tradition. As a child, she had been sickly and thought of herself as ugly. But neither her frailty nor her conviction about the way she looked kept her from being a happy child. Her father's library was filled with books. Reading had opened her eyes to other worlds. At first, her family was glad she had this escape. Poor girl, she wasn't healthy, and she wasn't pretty. She would not be asked to every party and ball. It was just as well she had found books. They could provide some escape for her.

Mary Anne loved her parents and she knew that they loved her. She knew too that she was a disappointment to them.

Even after she had outgrown the gaunt pinched look of her childhood, Mary Anne's family failed to see how attractive she had become.

By the time she was twenty-two years old, Mary Anne Read had read much of the great literature of the world. She could read in seven languages. Her mother and father began to worry about her future—what would become of their daughter? Most girls her age were married. By the time she reached the age of twenty-four, her parents accepted the fact that their daughter was a spinster. And although it was unusual for a girl in Mary Anne's class to leave home, they were almost relieved when she moved to Atlanta, Georgia, to become a librarian. Atlanta was not like Richmond. Perhaps she would meet someone there.

Mary Anne Read was happy in Atlanta. She enjoyed working with books, and her job left her time to read. Soon she began to review books for the Atlanta *Convention*. Her reviews attracted attention, at first locally, and then nationally. In those days, nationally meant H. L. Mencken and New York City. It was unusual for a young woman, a librarian, writing book reviews for a newspaper in Georgia, to attract attention in New York. But among the competent critics of the time, there were those who stood ready to welcome new and young talent. So it was that the young and gifted Mary Anne Read, librarian of Atlanta, Georgia, won quick recognition.

This recognition stimulated her.

Her urge to write was a natural development.

Mary Anne Read became a critic with some reputation. Even though she remained in Atlanta, her name began to appear in New York papers. Major publishers sent her advance copies of books to review and solicited her praise for book jackets. Several publishers tried to sound her out about a book. They invited her to come to New York. Among these publishers was Lemuel Herzog.

TWO

Lemuel Herzog was becoming the most exciting name in the book world. The firm had started as a partnership, Saunders & Herzog, but the partnership dissolved after two years. There could be but one boss; Lemuel Herzog bought out Saunders.

Lemuel Herzog was almost five feet ten inches tall but seemed shorter. He was a thin, dark man, with heavy Semitic features. He was almost homely, but beautiful women were attracted to him. Although he did not read much, he had a sixth sense for talent and ability, and he was willing to gamble on this sixth sense. He played the stock market, he backed plays. From the very beginning he had signed up talented and promising young writers as well as established authors. He spent money with an easy-handed nonchalance.

The Lemuel Herzog Publishing Company was located in a three-story gray house on East Fifteenth Street. The house had once been a private home and the rooms were big, with high ceilings. Lemuel Herzog had hired the most renowned designers to redecorate. Walls had been torn down. Bright modern colors contrasted with elegant marble fireplaces. There was a bar stocked with the finest whiskeys, and a private dining room for special luncheons. Rich sensuous carpets were on the floors, fine oil paintings on the walls. It was a showplace; an appropriate setting for the sensational publishing company it housed. Money flowed in. And flowed out. George Boorstein was the fifth young vice president to join the firm with an investment.

George Boorstein had come to New York from Philadelphia. He wanted to get into publishing and decided to buy his way in rather than work his way up. He had money to invest and would have prefered being one of the owners rather than an employee, but he was willing to do any kind of work to learn the ropes. He had no intentions of trying to dictate policy to men who knew the business better than he. His father had made money in department stores. It had been he who suggested to George that he buy a share of a publishing company to learn the business.

George Boorstein fitted into the way of things at the Lemuel Herzog Publishing Company quickly. He had not, when he first began, believed he could fit in so easily. He was not as up on books as some of the others; he knew this. But it was a nice congenial office and there were no cutthroat rivalries.

George Boorstein was ripe for experience. He was not stupid and he wanted to learn. He wanted to have good times as well. He liked parties. He liked meeting people who were famous, who were witty and clever, people who counted. He was invited to many parties. He knew that the money he spent had something to do with his popularity but knowing this did not trouble him. His purposes were suited; he was getting the gain. He wanted to be known. He planned to have his own publishing firm one day and being known and liked was creating future good will. Besides, he wanted experience, experience of much variety—including sex. There was no reason why a man should not have a good time as well as earn money.

It was not all fun at the Lemuel Herzog Publishing Company. The company was in business; and it did business. George Boorstein was serious about business. A man didn't invest money to lose it, not unless he was crazy. But he was there to learn, too. And to acquire experience, and a reputation. He knew he did not have whatever it took to achieve sensational goals but he believed he had enough intelligence to make a good living and to enjoy life. This was what he wanted. Good profits, good housing, good clothes, good food, good women, good books, good vacations, good friends, good times —a good life!

George Boorstein saw quickly that the Herzog Publishing Company offered a special kind of opportunity for him. He liked the environment. It was an exciting young world. Herzog himself was only thirty-two and he knew everybody worth knowing in the book world, almost everybody.

THREE

Mary Anne Read decided to go to New York for a short visit. When Lemuel Herzog received her note, he called in George Boorstein and told him to try to get her to sign a contract for a book.

"I'll do my best, Lemuel."

"I know that. I want the contract and the book," Lemuel Herzog said.

He smiled. George Boorstein smiled back. George knew that Lemuel Herzog was deadly serious about this Mary Anne Read. As much as Lemuel Herzog liked the role of big spender, man about town, and as much as he enjoyed knowing that people bragged about invitations to his parties and vied with each other for his attention, Lemuel Herzog knew that in order to sustain his reputation as a sensational publisher, he had to sign up bright new names as they appeared. Mary Anne Read was a bright new name.

George Boorstein could see that Lem was serious. Mary Anne Read would be a catch for the firm, no doubt about it. He had heard her name mentioned many times even though he himself had not read any of her book reviews or articles. He had heard that she was as beautiful as she was brilliant.

George had no illusions about himself; he was hardly the type that a beautiful and brilliant literary star would shine up to, but if Lemuel Herzog wanted him to try to sign her up, try he would.

"I'll do what I can, Lem."

"If she wants to get laid, lay her. If she doesn't, don't. But get her for the Herzog list."

"I'll do everything I can, Lem, but I can't swear that I'll get her before I've even laid eyes on her."

"I know that, George, but do what you can."
George Boorstein laughed.
"All right, Lem, I understand."
"Good luck."
"I might need it."
"Remember, don't let her give you her ass unless she'll give you her book, too."
"I'll try, Lem."

George Boorstein met Mary Anne Read that afternoon at a small reception given for her by Herzog Publishing Company. Within minutes, he was charmed by her Southern accent and her femininity. He watched her as she flirted and chattered with several of the other guests. He saw that she could shift in an instant to serious conversation about literature.

Within three hours after her arrival in New York City, Mary Anne Read had created a stir in the literary world.

After the party, twelve persons were invited to stay for dinner. It was the first time that George Boorstein had been invited to the inner circle. He was getting up in the world.

The dinner was for Mary Anne Read. Attention was focused on her. And she liked him. George Boorstein was aware of this from the very beginning. At one point, Lemuel Herzog had walked over to him. With his eyes on Mary Anne, Lem had asked him: "Will someone please tell me why there was a damned war with the South?"

"I'm sure I couldn't answer that question." George had laughed.

He watched Mary Anne. She was talking to Selwyn Richards. Suddenly, looking up, Mary Anne saw him watching her. She smiled at him. His hopes were stirred.

They saw each other every day. George was attracted to her. He began to look forward to going to bed with her.

In less than a week, George Boorstein knew that she felt the same attraction for him. He would have no problems; she would. He would just have to wait for the right moment.

But by the end of the week, George had doubts. Business mixed with pleasure could make business pleasant. It could also create difficulty. He didn't want to do anything to risk losing Mary Anne Read for the firm. And he wasn't sure that going to bed with an author was the best way to get her.

George pondered this as he put on his tuxedo. He would be seeing her in a few minutes. He'd have to follow his instincts.

When he left his apartment, George Boorstein had not decided. He wanted to go to bed with her but he was not a reckless man. Mary Anne was a new type for him; there was something very special about her. He wasn't the only one who thought so. He had heard Forman Dentz, who sat in the office next to his, talking about her. Forman had made no bones about envying George. Of course, Forman wanted to go to bed with any good-looking woman, and Mary Anne would be a real feather in his cap. But George Boorstein had an inside track; even Forman admitted this. Others felt this way, too, and George knew it.

Every important publisher in New York was after Mary Anne Read. He would be a laughing stock if some other publisher signed her up. He couldn't take a chance; he would have to concentrate on business in this case.

For one brief moment, George Boorstein stood still. In that split second he came as near as he ever would to realizing that his decision could be one that he would regret. In that delicate and feminine body of hers there was strength and purpose, intelligence—and a capacity for love.

And for a book that Lemuel Herzog wants to publish, he reminded himself, getting into a cab. He leaned back in the seat. Tonight was her last night in New York. He would have to get a commitment from her.

On the train returning to Atlanta, Mary Anne sat, a book in her lap. Why had she resisted making a commitment to George about her book? She intended to write one. And of the four publishers who had offered her contracts, she would rather sign with Herzog. Why hadn't she told George? He was so eager to have her say something about it. Was it because she was disappointed? Had she hoped he would talk about something more personal than the author-editor relationship he looked forward to?

As the train neared Atlanta, Mary Anne wrote a note to George Boorstein telling him that she had decided to accept a contract. She knew that he would write or telephone her. Maybe he would rush down to Atlanta.

Mary Anne was smiling as she stepped off the train.

Why hadn't George Boorstein written her? She'd been back two days. She had hoped he'd have written her even before he received her letter about the contract.

She had enjoyed New York; it was an exciting city. And she had met George there. She had met other men, some more interested in literature than he was, some more serious, but it was George Boorstein who had quickened her pulse rate when he walked into a room. And he had felt attracted to her. She was sure of it. Why hadn't he written? Not that she was blaming him. He was busy and she had just left New York two days ago. He'd spent so much time with her, his work must have piled up in his office. It was too soon to expect a letter. She couldn't have received one yet, not unless he'd rushed if off the same day that she left. Oh but if he had!

When old Sam Dodge rounded the corner at noon with the second mail delivery, Mary Anne felt excitement. But he did not stop. For a moment, she felt crushed. She turned from the window and walked back to her desk.

She was acting more like a silly school girl than a woman in love. A woman in love? But she couldn't mean this seriously; she didn't know George Boorstein well enough.

But she was in love with him.

There was one more mail delivery at three o'clock. Maybe she
would hear from him then. She was being silly. Tomorrow would
be the very soonest to expect a letter.

At three, Mary Anne was at the window. Again, Sam Dodge did
not stop. She turned. Suddenly she smiled.

—I'll act real, not like an F. Scott Fitzgerald character.

No letter came from George Boorstein the next day. Mary Anne
was more than disappointed; she felt dismissed. One minute she
would be angry, the next, she would try to be disdainful. Then
she'd tell herself to be patient, not to judge him until she knew
what had happened.

She spent a long, unhappy day.

No letter came the next day.

George Boorstein had no idea that Mary Anne Read was waiting
for a letter from him. He was a decent man but dull. And a dull
man is not deep, nor does he have imagination. He often accepts
the face of things as the spirit of what they are. There is much in
his life that he does not recognize.

George Boorstein had not written to Mary Anne because he
wanted to talk to Lemuel Herzog first about the contract they
would offer her. He could have offered her one on his own but he
preferred talking it over with Lem. And on the day that he received
the letter from Mary Anne telling him that she would be agreeable
to signing a contract with the Lemuel Herzog Publishing Company,
Lem was not in the office. George tried to see him on the next day
but Lem was tied up in meetings. And then there was a big party
and Lem hadn't come in until five the next day.

Finally, on the fourth day, George was able to see him.

"Thought I ought to talk with you about this first, Lem," George
said as he sat down by Lemuel Herzog's desk.

"What is it?"

"The contract for Mary Anne Read."

"You got her?"

"Yes," George answered and pushed her letter across the desk. "Here's the letter from her."

Lemuel Herzog smiled and took the letter. He was pleased. He wanted Mary Anne Read on his list and he'd gotten her.

"Did you send her a contract?"

"No, I wanted to talk it over with you first, Lem."

A frown flicked across Lemuel Herzog's face. George shouldn't have held up the contract. He'd been in this business long enough to know how sensitive authors were—especially women. He should have drawn it up and sent it to her. God knows what Mary Anne Read was thinking.

"I'm busy as a bee, George, you should have gone on with it. I'd have seen a copy of it. You shouldn't have held it up."

George felt Herzog's annoyance. He felt a little foolish. In a few minutes he left and proceeded with getting the contract drawn up.

Two days later, Mary Anne Read received a thick envelope from the Lemuel Herzog Publishing Company. At the end of a typed letter was typed "George Boorstein" with his signature over it. She looked in the envelope again and pulled out a contract. She turned back to the letter. She was more eager to read it than she was to read the contract.

We were glad to have received your letter...

Of course, the letter went on, he was glad on his own. He had not answered her sooner because even though he could have gone ahead and sent her a contract on his own, he'd decided it would be best to consult Mr. Herzog on it. Mr. Herzog had been out of the office for a day or so but he finally did get in to see him and Mr. Herzog had agreed to the terms that he, George, had proposed. There would be an advance of $2,000 upon signing the contract and an additional $1,000 each on the delivery of three books. There were two more sentences on the terms. One of the three books should be a novel. In her visit to New York, she had made a very good impression. They all hoped that she would return for another

visit soon; he himself would be especially pleased. And Mr. Herzog
wished for him to tell her how delighted he was to be adding her
name to the list of Herzog writers. If she had any questions, she was
to write him immediately. Yes, it was good that her name would be
on the Herzog list. He looked forward to hearing from her soon.
He ended the letter: ... *With warm regards.*

Mary Anne sat holding the letter in one hand and the contract
in the other. The look on her face was thoughtful. It was as if she
were moving from one place to another, one house to another. She
felt regret and anticipation, regret and expectation.

Later that day, Mary Anne signed the contract and had her signature notarized. She returned it with a cordial letter. She would be
returning to New York, she wrote. She didn't know exactly when
but she would be going back. And when she did, she would certainly let the Lemuel Herzog Publishing Company, and George
Boorstein, know.

She would not lose George Boorstein. Her mind was made up.

FOUR

Two days later, Mary Anne Read began work on a novel. It was a novel about a marriage. She didn't have a title for it yet but that could wait. She did not intend to start her career with the wrong book, one that would receive the acceptance accorded to a promising, young, but completely undeveloped talent.

Mary Anne Read had definite ideas about her career. These were not carefully thought out and planned; she had no model. But she did have a brain. She recognized problems as they developed, and she recognized solutions without going through preliminary stages of rational thought. Her intelligence was quick, her observations usually accurate. And her thinking clear.

One morning as she sat at her typewriter, she began to think of what she was writing. Suddenly she leaned forward and across the top of a blank page, she typed:

THE MORNING AFTER THE HONEYMOON.

That would be the title of her first book: *The Morning after the Honeymoon.*

She wrote to George Boorstein immediately about the title. And although she was eager for his reply, she did go on working on the book.

Five days after she had written, she received an answer from George Boorstein. It was on Herzog stationery. He had dictated the letter. Her title was very interesting, very, but some of them in the Herzog office were a little afraid that it might be too long. He had to confess that he was a bit on the dubious side, too. Of course there was plenty of time to settle on a title. It wouldn't be a bad idea for her to give some thought to a shorter one and then they could compare the two titles. He was, he wanted to assure her, de-

lighted to have heard from her. Not only was he glad but all of
them in the Herzog office were glad. It was exciting to all of them
to know that she was fully engaged in writing her first book and
that Herzog would have the honor and pleasure of publishing it.
He ended with *Most cordially*.

Then, a postscript:

> *I have jus talked with Halpern, who advises me that the*
> *check constituting your first advance on our contract*
> *will be mailed out to you tomorrow.*

> *GB*

Mary Anne had ripped the envelope open eagerly. Would he be
pleased with her title? Excited, maybe? Just as she had been. But
as she read, her excitement died. His words were so banal. She was
disappointed that her title had not been received with enthusiasm;
but this was not the main thing. The main thing was George Boorstein. She could no longer pretend anything else. She had had some
doubts even before she left New York. But she had hoped. Oh God
how she had hoped. She had shoved her doubts aside, but now she
had to face reality.

Mary Anne tried to write to George Boorstein. She made a start.
A second start. And then a third. It was hard. Hard, because even
knowing what she knew, she was in love with George Boorstein.
In fact, in openly admitting to herself that shortcomings existed, the
walls of her resistance crashed. She accepted as an axiom that in
order to love, hurt must be laid bare. Inner actions pressed upon
her. Inner warnings rang like bells in her head. George Boorstein
was the wrong man for her. But how could the man she loved be
the wrong man for her?

—Am I afraid to risk making a mistake?

The minute she asked herself this question, Mary Anne was able
to write:

> *My dear kind George:*
> *How wonderful—the contracts, your letter, the check.*

Now I can say, holding my head high, that I'm a Herzog
author. You are a wonder to pull it all through
for me, and to have done it so expeditiously. But my
dear new friend, I confess to you that I was disappointed
in your reaction to my title The Morning after the
Honeymoon. *My disappointment, needless to say, is*
inclusive and covers the others in the Herzog office
who are unsure about my title.
   Take my word for it, George, it's perfect.
And while I'm at it, you can take my word generally.
There's plenty of time for you all to change your
mind and agree with me. You'll see it my way.
   When I have more of The Morning after the
Honeymoon *written, perhaps I'll take another trip*
to New York. I know that you all will be agreeable
with me concerning my title. And my dear friend, you'll
find me agreeable.

                                        Fondly,
                                        Mary Anne

Mary Anne mailed her letter the next morning. A few hours later,
in the second mail of the day, she received another envelope from
the Herzog Publishing Company. This one contained the check
George had mentioned.

She was bursting with enthusiasm; she wanted to pitch into her
work. But four hours later, she was in a deep depression. She hadn't
been able to write a single sentence. A day that could never be again
was passing; it was almost gone.

There was no point in agonizing over time wasted. If she sat here
any longer, she *would* qualify as a character in an F. Scott Fitzgerald novel. She would read. She took down a book from a nearby
shelf.

In a little while, she was absorbed in *Mottka the Thief* by Sholom
Ashe. As she read, the thoughts that had been distressing and distracting her dropped from her mind.

It was quite late when she went to bed. She had finished the book. Mary Anne Read woke up a little before eight. Her mind was clear. She had finished, for this time at least, the kind of agonizing she had floundered in yesterday. Today would be much better.

Mary Anne wrote four and a half pages of her book. She found far more joy than torment in writing. But when her work was not going well, she felt miserable. On days when it did go well, days when she made progress, she was happy. Bad days were rare but they came with no forewarning. Or if there were any forewarnings, she didn't recognize them.

Gradually, a correspondence developed between Mary Anne Read and George Boorstein. She would write him of her progress and he would write in reply. Several times he wrote that he was becoming increasingly enthusiastic about her book and that he was impressed by her progress, as were the others in the Herzog offices. When was she coming to New York?

Mary Anne wanted to pay another visit to New York. She remembered her last trip with nostalgia. It had been a good trip but the next one would be even better. At times she had a strong desire to pack up and make the trip immediately but she didn't act upon these impulses. It would be better if she waited until more of her book was written. As exciting and stimulating as New York City was, it could be distracting, too. And she had accepted an advance for her book. She could take no chances on not delivering it. No, it wouldn't be wise to take time out from her work now. In all likelihood, she would be wined and dined again, praised and flattered as she had been on her last trip. Then if something went wrong, if her book came out the wrong way, it could seem that she had gone to New York, posed as a writer, and that it was all fakery.

This is how Mary Anne rationalized. Although she subconsciously knew that she was an artist and accepted the fact that her work was at this point the most important part of her life, she was a young and attractive woman who had met a man she was attracted to as she had never been attracted before. Because she had yet to write her first novel, Mary Anne was too modest to say that her work was more important to her than love. This is why her rationalizations sometimes bordered on the banal. And she wasn't sure about her feelings for George Boorstein. These feelings were expectations of the future placed in the present. They were for what had not come to be. They were preludes to their own meaning and fulfillment. Out of these, both yearning and doubts had emerged. She would not go to New York for George Boorstein until her novel was written—at least to the extent that it was a certainty.

Mary Anne Read discovered, forgetting that she had already known this, that it was harder to write fiction than it was to write an essay. She could only work on her novel for three or four hours a day. At the end of that time, she was tired. On some days, she could only manage a single page. She was not making the progress she should. When would she finish it? At this rate it would be years.

Mary Anne would become impatient at times but she knew that she could not hurry her writing. She was writing the only way she could. She had expected some bad moments when she decided to write a novel.

As frustrating as blocks were, Mary Anne did make steady progress. And she wrote to George Boorstein about it. His answers were always encouraging. Sometimes when reading his letters, she would smile. His trying to encourage her as a writer was funny, almost pathetic. She didn't need encouragement. But still, she treasured his letters. They encouraged her in other ways. They encouraged her to believe that George Boorstein cared.

One day, Mary Anne took the pages she had written off a shelf in her workroom. It was a considerable pile. She went through them. She didn't read every word on every page but she skimmed over much of it. There were 300 pages written. Half of *The Morning after the Honeymoon* had been completed.

Excitedly, she wrote a long letter to George Boorstein. Then she sat back in her chair and imagined him receiving it. He would smile boyishly, jump up from his desk, and march in to Lemuel Herzog with it.

—Look at this, Lem, from Mary Anne.

Lemuel Herzog would take the letter and read it.

—Looks damned promising, George.

—It certainly does; she's a talented young woman, Lem.

—Talented? She's brilliant!

Mary Anne frowned. Lemuel Herzog was quick and had a sharp and aggressive mind. His insight was sharp. In addition to all this, he had a dramatic and theatrical flare. He acted his real life as though it were a play written for him. He was an intelligent man, she knew this, but he was more quick than intelligent. His mind worked well because he was a man practically without inhibitions. This was obvious in matters of literature. He had judgment; but he had no taste. He was too intelligent to misjudge anything that was obviously poor. Were this man to call her brilliant, she would have grounds for being pleased. But the point was that she had no need to be so praised by Lemuel Herzog. Brilliant was a relative word. Its meaning was relative. It might be that she was brilliant but Lemuel Herzog saying it made her neither more nor less brilliant than she was.

Mary Anne smiled. Why all this reflection? Lemuel Herzog hadn't called her brilliant. George hadn't even received the letter in front of her, much less jumped up from his desk to take it in to Lemuel Herzog. She had been daydreaming. And all of her daydreaming about Lemuel Herzog had nothing to do with him; it had to do with George Boorstein. When George received her letter, he probably would go to talk to Lemuel Herzog about it. George would think that Lemuel would be interested that she was halfway through the first book. And then, perhaps, Lemuel Herzog would say something that would make George proud of her.

FIVE

She completed the first draft. She didn't want anyone else to see it until she went over it again. She had some doubts about the final section. She might have to do some editing there. But first, she needed a vacation.

She would go to New York. She would stay a week or two. There was no reason why she shouldn't stay longer should she decide to. But she wouldn't stay longer than a month. That was definite.

George Boorstein was waiting for her at Pennsylvania Station. She hadn't seen him at first and felt panic.

—If he doesn't come?

Then she saw him.

"George!"

She ran to him, opened her arms, and kissed him spontaneously.

"Oh I'm so glad to see you," she said.

Her eyes were bright. She looked up at him, all smiles and softness.

George Boorstein was surprised. He hadn't expected such a welcome. He moved toward her again but checked himself. There were other things to do. He must attend to her baggage and get through the crowd on the platform. He would have to find a cab to get her to the Algonquin, where he had reserved a suite for her.

"I'm so happy to be here, George."

"And I'm happy that you're here," he told her.

He was happy, he realized, but he couldn't just stand there. He had to find a porter. He looked around. He was charmed by her chatter but only heard part of what she was saying in the noisy scene.

Finally, with a bit of pride at how he had taken command of the situation, he took her elbow and led her behind a porter toward an exit.

At the Hotel Algonquin, George Boorstein stepped up to the front desk and said that a reservation had been made for Miss Mary Anne Read.

The man behind the desk looked at his register. Yes, indeed, a reservation had been made. For a suite. With this, he pushed the register across the counter. Mary Anne signed it, turned, and started toward the elevator. George, walking beside her, said that he would give her a chance to freshen up and rest after her long trip, and that he would telephone her later about dinner.

She turned, a look of surprise on her face. Wasn't he coming up with her to see what kind of suite she was getting? George Boorstein smiled with restraint. Of course he would.

He rode up in the elevator beside her. The two of them followed the porter to the suite. After the porter had been tipped and left, closing the door behind him, Mary Anne Read and George Boorstein made love.

There was a Herzog party that night for Mary Anne. There were beautiful women there, and intelligent women, and some, like Mary Anne Read, who were both beautiful and intelligent. There were men there, too, men reputed to be brilliant. There were many literary names. At first Mary Anne was shy. She wished the party hadn't been given. She would have preferred being alone with George. Or even alone to let herself discover what this afternoon in the hotel suite meant.

But as the party got along and the liquor flowed, Mary Anne was no longer sorry to be there. There was good conversation. She was practically surrounded all evening. She had scarcely more than a dozen words with George Boorstein but they kept seeking each other out with their eyes.

—I'm so happy to be here and to be in love!

Lemuel Herzog caught the look on Mary Anne's face as she looked at George. He smiled. He wished that he had had the time to cultivate this Southern blossom. But there were more days to come.

Mary Anne was thinking of the days to come, too. Would there be many other days of her life as happy as this one had been? Could there be?

—And today is not over!

She smiled to herself.

It was late. Soon after Lemuel Herzog left, other guests began to leave. The party began to break up. Mary Anne caught George's eyes. He nodded in agreement. Casually, he drifted to her side and told her that they could leave in about ten minutes without attracting undue attention. Fifteen minutes later, they stood in front of the building looking for a cab.

"It was a good party, wasn't it, Mary Anne?"

"Oh yes, darling, a wonderful party."

"Yes it was, a good party."

"Darling George, it was not the party, it was you."

"And you, dear."

They laughed.

"Mary Anne, dear?"

"Yes?"

"We would be far more comfortable at my place than in your hotel."

"You're the lord and master," Mary Anne said.

He hugged her. Then, walking to the curb, he tried to hail a cab.

"We'll get one soon," he said.

George Boorstein was as decent as he was dull, but his dullness was more evident than his decency. Mary Anne tried to avoid rec-

ognizing her superiority. What was superiority? Why did it matter if one or another of two lovers was superior? There was no absolute superiority. If you were superior in one direction, you could
very well not be superior in another direction. And if you were
superior to your beloved, it meant that you had more to give him.
To love was to give and it should be a joy to be able to give more.

Mary Anne Read loved George Boorstein. They made love every day. There was harmony between them. But would it stay this
way? Were she to marry him, would her superiority cause disil-
lusionment? Of course, he hadn't spoken of marriage. But she believed he had thought about it. She knew, and she knew that George
Boorstein knew, that what had flamed up between them was extra-
ordinary. Their lovemaking was full of joy.

But there were other questions she would have to face. George
Boorstein was a Jew. She had never known many Jews, certainly
none intimately. In fact, this was the problem. George's being Jewish did not bother her nearly so much as the fact that she knew
nothing about Jews. Would his being Jewish make it harder for
her to know him better? Understand him? Would it be a wall between them?

Mary Anne looked at the clock. It was almost nine o'clock. She
got out of bed and went in to take a shower.

After three weeks in New York, Mary Anne decided to return
to Atlanta. She gave her work as the reason. It was a reason but not
the only reason. She could have worked in New York; it would
have been harder but she could have done it.

Mary Anne cried on the train taking her back. She wished that
she had stayed. But she couldn't. She had to leave. She was weak.
Tired. Fatigued. Mary Anne had not felt so exhausted since the days
of her girlhood when she had lain in bed for days. She knew that
if she had remained in New York, she would have become ill. She
could not have gone on at such a hectic pace. There were parties
almost daily. And there was George Boorstein. Their lovemaking

had been a daily event. Would she suffer from wanting him? Would she be jealous? She could not be sure how she would feel a few days from now. All that she could be sure of was that she could not have gone on that way unless she wanted to be a stupid and inexcusably silly young woman. She would have made herself sick. The sensible thing was to return to Atlanta and to finish her book.

Knowing this, she continued to weep on the train.

SIX

She scanned the page again. What was wrong with her? She had read this page three times. Why couldn't she get back into her work? She had not expected to get off the train from New York and sit down on her first day in Atlanta to work. But she'd been back for almost a week. Why was she still so restless?

Mary Anne knew why. It was because of George Boorstein. She was in love with him and she missed him. Being away from him was torment. But there was another reason for her restlessness. She was afraid she would lose him. During her three weeks in New York, she had seen that George traveled in a group with many attractive and intelligent young women. In his position, he met new women every week.

She wrote him long letters. When he answered, his letters were matter-of-fact. She reminded herself that he was not a writer, that he was a businessman; but this did not help. It never occurred to her that it was her letters that hindered him. She wrote with such sensibility, so beautifully, that he became self-conscious when he sat down to write her.

Were Mary Anne Read writing a story about a love between two characters, one like George Boorstein and the other like herself, she would have perceived this. But she was not writing a story about it, she was living it. And her emotions flooded over her understanding. She did not stop to think about her own emotions, and her vanity and pride were wounded.

At first, George Boorstein loved receiving her letters. They were so beautifully written. But what could he say in reply? He would start a letter, tear it up, start a second one, tear that up too, and go on like this for a half hour. Finally he would give up. Then the unwritten letter became an unfulfilled task.

The matter of letters was distressing. If he didn't answer her, she would be hurt and think God knows what. If he did, his letters would seem so ordinary that she would be disappointed. He could only write dull letters. What would she think?

Then his common sense would come to the rescue. He would remind himself that he was a man in love. Well, infatuated, at least. They didn't know each other too well, not really. He was drawing things out in an attenuated way, making matters overimportant. Overimportant in the wrong way:

Once rescued by his common sense, George Boorstein would sit down and write a quick, short note.

After receiving such a note one day, Mary Anne sat down and started to write. She was clear and excited. Her work was coming right. Her vacation had been good for her; it had left her refreshed. She wrote for several hours. Her face was flushed with pleasure when she stopped. If she continued at this pace, she would finish the book sooner than she had expected.

Mary Anne attributed her streak of writing to her love for George. But she knew better. What she was writing had been crystallizing in her unconscious mind for years. She had achieved command of her experience. She remembered Bergson. She was having a sudden leap. She had been struck by his observation about sudden leaps of intuition when she had read it. Now she was having an inexplicable leap of writing. Falling in love with George might have something to do with it; it could have been a catalyst. She certainly did not resent giving him credit but neither would she think about her writing as a schoolgirl.

After four weeks at this pace, Mary Anne was exhausted. She felt spent. She did not sleep well. She had always had some trouble sleeping and attributed this to her naps during the day. Even after she became a librarian, she always napped for an hour when she came home from work. She tired easily. Sometimes the nap would stretch out to two hours. On such days, it was hard to sleep when her bedtime came. She had, from time to time, resorted to the phenobarbital the doctor had prescribed. She had resisted this until her doctor scolded her: "Come, come, Mary Anne, you're a sensible young woman. Do you think for one moment that I'd recommend the use of a sedative if I thought you were acting the Southern belle with imaginary maladies? Why I hardly pick up a magazine that I don't read about the work you're doing. You're a busy young woman and you need your rest. You've always tended to being a fragile little thing. You must get your rest; not only for your work but for your health, too."

Mary Anne stopped resisting the pills. She depended on them. She couldn't sleep otherwise and yet she knew that the sleep they gave her was not always refreshing. Some mornings she woke feeling dull and lethargic. Her brain, even her features, felt thickened and dulled by the pills. She would force herself out of bed. And then she would force herself to sit down at her desk and write. Only after she worked for an hour or so would she feel alive and alert.

Mary Anne began to channel all her energy toward her work. She saw less and less of her friends. She wrote fewer letters and she put less into the letters she did write. George Boorstein's letters required little in reply; but even if they'd been different, she could not have maintained the emotional tone of her earlier letters.

The Morning after the Honeymoon was absorbing all her emotional and intellectual energy. Mary Anne Read had entered into a race with time. She had not consciously realized this yet. All she knew was that her stay in New York, exciting as it had been, had exhausted her. And that it was taking her a long time to get back her strength.

For the first time, Mary Anne Read faced the fact that her energy and her strength had limits. This being the case, her work would take priority over everything else. Everything.

SEVEN

It was finished. She would take the manuscript to New York herself. It had been six months since she had seen George Boorstein. No. She was too spent to make the trip. She was simply not up to the rounds of parties, the meetings and dates. She mailed the manuscript to George Boorstein.

EIGHT

THE MORNING AFTER THE HONEYMOON
by Mary Anne Read, New York, 1929
Lemuel Herzog Publishing Co., 373 Pgs. $2.50

*Mary Anne Read comes upon the American literary scene
with some of the highest credentials. None other than
H. L. Mencken, the Baltimore sage who has an eye, ear,
nose plus a sixth sense for new young writers has signed these
credentials for Miss Read. She is good, "on the highest
authority" in the Kingdom of Letters. As if to attach a privy
seal, her fellow Virginian, James Branch Cabell, has
affixed his signature to her papers of certification.*

*A thing about Miss Read, however, is the fact that she
is her own best credential.*

*Mary Anne Read is not yet known to the general reading
public but I wager that this will be changed, thanks to*
The Morning after the Honeymoon. *She has been known
to some of us for a number of years (even though she is still
a young woman), due to her informed, casually erudite,
and finely discriminating book reviews, which appear
regularly in the Atlanta* Convention. *She moves with
Southern grace through the literature of other countries.
Some of us have long been expecting her first book. Our
vigil has not been in vain. It ends with the rewarding gift
of one of the most remarkable first novels that it has been
my good fortune to review.*

The Morning after the Honeymoon *is a novel that
conveys the truth of the heart of a young woman, who, only
yesterday, was a girl. Frances Andrews returns to her home*

*in Richmond with her husband. It is her bridal home and
they have been on their honeymoon. It was a happy one.
The setting is for the kind of marriage and life often
designated as "happily ever after." One morning Frances
Andrews wakes up before her husband. She looks at the
handsome sturdy young man beside her and thinks that from
that moment on, her life, her happiness, her joy and sorrow,
all that she is, will depend upon him.*

*This is how Mary Anne Read sets her story. It would
seem to be an almost banal and unoriginal beginning.
But Miss Read magically creates this situation as though
Frances Andrews were the first bride. Indeed, she endows
this banal situation with the shock of originality. And the
entire novel is a fulfillment of the promise of the opening.*

*This is a brilliant first novel of healthy realism. No one
who reads* The Morning after the Honeymoon *can
doubt that it heralds the beginning of a bright new literary
career.*

Henry Deak's review was just one of the favorable notices that
The Morning after the Honeymoon received. The praise was far
beyond all her hopes. Mary Anne had tried to steel herself against
being hurt or distressed should her book be attacked. She knew
she could withstand adverse criticism if it were stupid and ignorant,
or mean and vicious. But her reaction to the criticism would depend
upon what it was, and the source. She believed she could withstand
any unfavorable reviews. So she told herself. She knew that she
should not allow herself to be troubled by hostile judgments.

Mary Anne had told herself all this in order to prepare for whatever happened, but she maintained a strong confidence about the
fate of her book.

Her book was liked. Liked more than bought.

Mary Anne went to New York a week before publication. She

had rested a lot after finishing the book and felt stronger than she
had in months. George Boorstein met her at Pennsylvania Station.

Mary Anne was still in love with George Boorstein but she was
not sure he was in love with her.

He kissed her when they met and said that he was glad to see her,
very glad. She was happy to see him, too, she said. She was happy,
but she was apprehensive, also.

—Maybe . . .

She did not complete her thought.

"Are these all your bags, dear?" he asked.

"Yes, that's all."

George Boorstein got a porter and led her to a taxicab. Once more
he took her to the Algonquin.

The response to her book surpassed all their expectations. Even
Lemuel Herzog was impressed. The stay in New York should have
been the happiest, the most glamorous of all her visits. But this was
not the case. Not that it was unhappy or disastrous. It wasn't that at
all. It was just, and Mary Anne would only admit this to herself, that
it was a denouement. Her book was what mattered to her. In it, she
had written some of the edge off her own disappointment in love.
She had encompassed the relationship of unity and dependency in
love and marriage. In her characterization of the young bride,
Frances Andrews, Mary Anne had also encompassed the urge to grow
and the impulses involved in the individuality in a human being, even
a young bride in love with her husband. She had written of a woman in love and described the development of this woman's consciousness which, although reflected from sexual experience with her
husband, could grow into conflict with that husband and then have
only one end—disaster. In writing this story, Mary Anne had imag-
inatively lived through love. The story was not based on any personal experience of her own, nor was it a forecast of her own expectations. Mary Anne Read had created her story but from it, she
had expanded her resources of feeling. She had not done this consciously.

Mary Anne was disappointed. Had she expected too much? Had she anticipated the impossible? Was what she hoped for beyond getting, out of reach of experience? She had a feeling of emptiness. It was something she couldn't get away from. And this feeling robbed her of enjoyment and satisfaction. Perhaps, she told herself, it was a letdown after the long spurt of creative effort in writing *The Morning after the Honeymoon*. She had worked at a steady pace for those last weeks; it was only natural to feel this way now. The parties, the conversation, the flattery. What did they matter?

Many of those who remembered her vivaciousness, her sparkling brilliance, and her Southern coquettishness, noticed the difference in her. George Boorstein did. He wondered if it had to do with him. Whether it did or didn't, he didn't like it. Others would think it was his fault. He knew he had been a source of envy because of his affair with Mary Anne. She was young, beautiful, and one of the most promising new writers on the literary horizon. But now, she was inclined to remain silent, to sit as if she barely heard what was being said around her. Some were saying that he had crushed her spirit and this got under his skin. Mary Anne was not responsible for the gossip, he realized this, but still he began to resent her. His feelings toward her cooled. It had been obvious to him for a long time that he could only play second fiddle in her life. And he harbored no desire to take second place to a book, not even a Lemuel Herzog best seller.

The more he thought about these things, the more resentment he felt. Finally, he decided that it was a "no-go" with him and Mary Anne Read. Theirs could not be a permanent relationship. Sooner or later it would have to end.

On the train, returning to Atlanta, Mary Anne came to the conclusion that she should not have gone to New York. It was not the city itself, nor anything the Lemuel Herzog Publishing Company had done, nor was it due to George Boorstein. It was her, Mary Anne Read. She had gone to New York at the wrong time. She was spiritually lethargic. She simply didn't have the strength to be gay, flirtatious, or clever. She could not trip any of New York's light fantastics. She was in a very low key. She kept feeling it was all an encore. She had seen the same people before, said the same things before, heard the same things before. The wonder and shine of the new was gone. She must have been a burden to poor George at times. She hadn't even been able to pretend to be interested when they were with groups. She had not measured up to George's expectations, she was sure of this. Mary Anne was starting to think that what George found most attractive in her was her attractiveness to other men in the New York literary circle.

Well it was over. The trip was over. And she was on her way back to Atlanta. Back to her work.

Once there, Mary Anne was somewhat amused about her musings. She felt sure that others didn't realize what a fiasco the trip had been.

NINE

M ary Anne Read began a new novel. But the work went slowly. She had trouble conceiving scenes and kept going off on tangents. This went on for several days. Finally, she put it aside. She would do something that she had been thinking of for a long time—an anthology of short stories from *Aesop's Fables* to James Joyce's *Dubliners*. She would write a general introduction and then make comments on each of the stories.

Having made up her mind, Mary Anne became enthusiastic. She started reading and rereading stories. She read in chronological order, starting with *Aesop's Fables* and the Bible. She wanted to study the changes and innovations in short stories.

It was a happy period. She was completely immersed in her work. As the book began to take shape, she thought of George Boorstein. She missed him. What had gone wrong during this last trip? There had been signals, if not of a rupture, at least of the beginnings of one. It was subtle but she was perceptive. Things weren't the same between them. She hoped that whatever it was could be repaired. She didn't want to lose George Boorstein. But if she did, she would have to experience it.

Well thank heavens she was calm about this possibility; she was acting like an adult about George Boorstein for a change.

But there was no reason why she shouldn't be calm. The rupture had not happened, she'd only thought of it as a possibility. Whether or not she could remain calm in the face of a severance between them remained to be seen. She did not want it to happen; she would be hurt. She knew this.

Was she going to go through the farce all over again? The melodrama of waiting for letters from George Boorstein? It seemed that she was. Why couldn't she control herself? She should be able to; she was doing work that absorbed her. But it didn't absorb her to such an extent that she could refrain from acting the part of a schoolgirl.

Half laughing, Mary Anne resumed her reading for the anthology.

Even though *The Morning after the Honeymoon* received favorable reviews, sales did not reach the expectations of the Lemuel Herzog Publishing Company. They expected sales to run between five and ten thousand copies. And now they weren't sure that it would go to twenty-five hundred, which was the break-even figure.

Lemuel Herzog was disappointed.

Mary Anne Read was disappointed, too, but she didn't feel that the book's not selling meant she had failed. Or that the book itself was a failure from the standpoint of its conception or the way it was written. She did not accept the sales as a criticism of her work.

From the very beginning, Mary Anne Read had written more letters to George Boorstein than she had received from him. But now his letters had slackened off to such a degree that she restrained herself from writing him as often as she wanted to. She missed him terribly. She did not want the affair to end. She knew that they were different in temperament and that his interest in literature was limited, almost restricted. He was not unintelligent; he could understand some works of literature but it didn't seem to matter to him. What he understood didn't affect his inner life. George Boorstein was insensitive to the power of art, even art that he understood.

Mary Anne knew that their differences related to how they responded to the qualities of living.

And yet, she wanted him.

What was the matter with her? She had work to do. She picked up *The Satyricon of Petronius* in Latin.

Mary Anne made progress in the preparation of her anthology. It was important for her work to do this anthology now. She knew this. And she knew that they did not understand at the Herzog office. George had written her:

> *Here, we all believe that a talent like yours*
> *should not be wasted or delayed in its develop-*
> *ment by applying itself to a secondary work.*
> *We can find all the persons we want, with plenty*
> *to spare, who can edit an anthology. But we cannot*
> *find another Mary Anne Read so easily.*

Mary Anne suspected that this was the general attitude at Herzog and not solely George's own personal view. Nevertheless, the letter irritated her. She knew that it was ridiculous, that she should be able to laugh it off. She had long known that publishers never hesitated to give writers advice about their work. But she couldn't laugh it off. She wrote a sharp letter to George reminding him that she, Mary Anne Read, was a writer and a critic and that most of the members of the Herzog Publishing Company were neither. Under the circumstances, it could be assumed that she possessed some understanding of how a writer goes about his or her career.

It was a blasting letter. Mary Anne tore it up.

Mary Anne Read ended her anthology with a Sherwood Anderson story. Many of her selections were familiar and had been anthologized frequently but her comments made the anthology unusual. She pointed out that in the present era, techniques have grown rapidly and that human emotions cannot expand in the same way. Therefore, modern writers must make their own form. She cited Chekhov as an example.

She sent the anthology off to the Lemuel Herzog Publishing Company. With the anthology out of the way, she began to think that she might go to Europe. She didn't want to go to New York

again and she needed to get away for a while. She would return
fresher to start her new novel.

—A trip to Paris with George.

What a wonderful trip that would be!

Mary Anne was awaiting word from him about his reactions and
the reactions of the others in the office to her anthology. She reminded herself that they had been less than enthusiastic about her
decision to do the anthology before she started her new novel. She
should not be too disappointed if their reaction was not good.

But she knew that she would be.

The following week, George Boorstein wrote informing her that
the opinions in the office were mostly on the side of the anthology.
It was a superb job she had done. Herzog would bring out the book,
The matter of permissions had to be attended to but he himself
would do this for her.

Mary Anne wrote back immediately. It gave her great joy to
know that George had responded so favorably to her anthology.
And needless to say, it gave her joy to learn that others at Herzog
were favorable to the work. Their responses, and especially his,
George's, were in themselves sufficient reward for her work. But
again, needless to say, she was willing to accept other rewards
should they come in due course.

Mary Anne added that she had been thinking about her next novel but she had not definitely decided whether to start it immediately or wait and go to Europe for a month or two. Paris had been in
her thoughts of late. It had been years since she'd been there. Could
he take a vacation at this time? He could go to Paris with her.
Would he like to? She would love to be in Paris with him and show
him the places she loved and enjoyed.

She had no sooner mailed the letter than she regretted it. She
was leaving herself open to rejection. She shouldn't have done it.
But why not? Why shouldn't she let him know that she wanted to
go to Paris and would like it if he came along? All she'd done was
ask him if he cared to make the trip with her. There was nothing
to regret.

But she did regret sending the letter.

George Boorstein wrote that he was very sorry but that he could not take the time off to go to Paris with her. He thanked her for thinking of him. It was a splendid and generous thought on her part and he only wished he could avail himself of the opportunity but it was out of the question at the present time.

The letter hurt. But there was more than hurt in her reaction. Mary Anne Read was not accustomed to being turned down. It was humiliating. He probably didn't realize that it was. His lack of sensitivity was an asset at times like these. If he didn't realize it, then she was less humiliated.

Why was she sitting here measuring her humiliation? It didn't matter whether or not she was humiliated. He had rejected her and she didn't like it. Period. There was no need to read all sorts of meanings in it. She would go to Paris alone.

TEN

Mary Anne Read sailed from New York. George Boorstein saw her off. She stood at the crowded rail of the liner as tug boats towed it into the Hudson River. She could still see him on the pier. She loved him. It was crowded on deck. People were laughing and talking at friends. She had never felt so alone.

The trip across the Atlantic was pleasant. At first, Mary Anne spent most of her time alone resting and reading. But after a few days, she met some of the other passengers. She played shuffleboard. She danced. She enjoyed the crossing.

By the time she arrived on the boat train at the Gare St. Lazarre in Paris, Mary Anne Read was looking forward to her stay. She was in a gay mood. But her gay moods were conditioned by undercurrents of sadness. Mary Anne Read could be gay but she was not a gay person.

Her first enthusiasm about being back in Paris quickly diminished. She tired too easily. After an hour or so of sightseeing, she would have to rest. Sometimes she sat at a cafe with a glass of wine but sometimes she was so depleted she had to return to her hotel for a nap. On some days, she was too tired to leave her hotel at all. She had no energy, no strength. Something was wrong with her. She didn't think it was anything serious. She was probably just run down. But she shouldn't try to do too much; she must get lots of rest. Of course her mental attitude might have something to do with her feeling of fatigue. She was disappointed in George Boorstein.

She brooded over him far too much. He could have come to Paris with her had he wanted to.

Mary Anne woke up one morning to see the sun spreading through the hotel room. She called down for breakfast. It was going to be a beautiful day. She had had a good night's sleep. She felt rested. There was a knock on the door.
"Entree, s'il vous plait."
A waiter entered with breakfast. *"Bon jour, madame."* He set the tray down on the desk. Mary Anne signed for the breakfast, reached for her bag and took out some change.
"Merci, monsieur."
"Merci, madame."
He left. Mary Anne looked at her breakfast. It looked good. Her day was starting. It was going to be a lovely one, she knew it already.

It had been an almost perfect day. Mary Anne had walked around Paris. No streets in the world were so interesting, she thought. She had walked in the Jardin de Luxembourg. She loved this garden, she always had, but never more than she did today. Then she walked along the quais, looking at books in the stalls. And there was the Cathedral of Notre Dame, gray and old and solid in the sunlight. A massive creation of the past, a voice of the past, that had endured. Hundreds of years before the name Mary Anne Read, George Boorstein, Lemuel Herzog, or even the United States of America had been thought of, conceived, or known, this monument of beauty and aspiration had been created. Napoleon had formally become emperor within its walls. He made his Josephine empress of France here. Many historic events had taken place in the cathedral; but the cathedral itself was history.

That night, Mary Anne had dinner with friends, the Colstons. Tom and Jane had taken her to a small restaurant on the Ile St. Louis that they had discovered. It was very pleasant. She liked them both;

they were an attractive couple and intelligent. Tom came from Richmond, Jane from Baltimore. Tom was a historian and he taught at the University of Virginia. There was some money in the Colston family and Tom and Jane spent their summers traveling. After dinner, they walked to the Champs Elysses and sat late at Fougets. It had been a delightful evening, a perfect ending to a good day.

There were other good days in Paris.

Mary Anne went back to the Cemetery Pere La Chaisse. She climbed the hill to the gates very slowly but she was still tired when she reached them. She was breathing heavily. The climb had been an effort, more of an effort than she thought it would be. She could feel her heart pounding inside her chest. She was out of breath; she had to sit for a while.

When her breathing had returned to normal, Mary Anne strolled through the cemetery looking at the crowded, chilling headstones and statues. So much jumbled up stone and marble. In memoriam. And inside the vaults, under the ground, were the bones of the dead of centuries past. The cemetery was awesome.

Mary Anne stopped frequently to read the names on the headstones. It was a poor memorial—a name in marble over a mound of dirt. How sad. But no one could change it.

She looked at the grave of Heloise and Abelard. She was stirred. Death was cruel. But here were the graves of a few whose lives had counted in the history of the human race.

Mary Anne wandered about the cemetery for two hours. She felt the beauty as deeply as she felt the silence. The sadness of death was softened by the beauty. Finally she left. She looked down over the city. She thought of Balzac's Rastignac shaking his fist at Paris. An impulsive gesture of youth.

Mary Anne's visit to the cemetery had stirred her. The time of life was short when measured against the time of recorded history. After living a short life, most people died and were forgotten. Only a few were remembered. Everyone couldn't be. She wanted to be.

This was not just a wish; it was a goal.

Mary Anne cut her trip short. She was tired so much of the time that it was depressing. It was more than depressing, it was frightening. Especially when she was lying, almost exhausted, in her hotel room. If she should become ill here, she would be alone. And suppose she were seriously ill? What if she should die over here?

Mary Anne decided to return to America.

The voyage was restorative. Mary Anne felt much stronger by the time the liner neared New York harbor. She should have stayed in Paris a little longer, and gone on to Rome. All she had needed was a few days of good rest. Well, it was silly to think of this now. She would go back another time. Returning sooner than she planned was no disaster. Coming back to America was always a thrill. She stood by the rail, looking out over the ocean for that first sight of land. She began to feel excited. She had cabled George; he would meet her.

The ocean was calm. The sun streaked the surface of the water. It was a magnificent view. She looked toward land. She still could not see it. She was eager to see George, to spend some time in New York. But then she wanted to go home and get down to work. Her new novel. And she wanted to translate the poems of Jules LaForgue.

"Land!"

Mary Anne heard a passenger cry out. She looked. Far off, through a light haze, she saw the dock line. It was not much more than a pencil line in the distance. Mary Anne was filled with emotion. It was land, the land of her country. She was moved. She was coming home to America. Tears came to her eyes. She was embarrassed, but only for a second. There was no reason why she should feel apologetic or try to make excuses. It was good to come home.

Mary Anne started getting impatient for the ship to dock. Every moment seemed painfully long. Down on the pier, there was a crowd. Many waved up at the passengers standing by the rail. Mary Anne saw George. She called to him but her voice was lost in the

noise. He did not hear her. Mary Anne watched him, hoping that
he would look up in her direction. She didn't want to keep calling
him; she felt foolish.

The ship edged against the dock. People were waving and shouting. The ship's band started playing "The Star-Spangled Banner."
Now George saw her. His face broke into a smile and he waved.
She waved back and blew him a kiss. He kept looking up at her,
smiling and waving, blowing kisses and calling up to her. But she
couldn't hear what he was saying. As she looked down at him,
she thought again of how much she loved him.

Mary Anne rushed to his arms outside the customs gate. In the cab
on the way to the Hotel Algonquin, she kissed him passionately.
With him beside her, she registered at the hotel. She started toward
the elevator, assuming that he would come with her. He hesitated.

"Aren't you coming up?"

"Yes if I'm invited," he answered slowly.

"Darling, you need no invitation," she said, speaking softly.

"Of course I'll come up, Mary Anne."

For a moment she had the feeling that he agreed to come up because he didn't want to hurt her feelings.

She flung this impression from her mind.

A bellboy took them to the suite. After George tipped him, he
left them alone. They looked at each other. Mary Anne looked
beautiful, as beautiful as he had ever seen her. There was a sensuality
in her face, and a sadness. George smiled. Then suddenly, struck by
her beauty and the sadness he saw, he felt a strange premonition.

She walked into his arms. They made love.

George Boorstein seemed happy to see her. He was almost un-
prosaic for the first couple of days. But George was a businessman.
His mind focused on business and other considerations were sec-
ondary. His emotions and his feelings were kept in separate com-

partments. There was much matter-of-factness about George Boorstein.

But she had been aware of this before. It was no surprise. Why did she allow herself to be disappointed? After all, she knew George Boorstein more intimately than she knew any other living man. Even though she might wish he could be something else, she couldn't blame him for being what he was. Or for her own disappointment. He had never pretended to be anything else. And it was not a new disappointment. It was the same one she had felt from the beginning of their affair.

Mary Anne knew that their relationship had passed its peak. Still, she could not give him up. Theirs was not a permanent relationship, she knew this. But it would be too distressing to force the issue at this point. And she would be leaving New York in a week. She would then get on a train, return to Atlanta, and begin work on her new book. There was no need to force the issue now. There was nothing brave about her attitude. She had no obligation to be brave. She could not afford to let herself be torn apart at this time. It was not good at any time but now she was bent on beginning her new novel.

They made love every day.

At the end of the week, Mary Anne kissed George Boorstein goodbye before she boarded the train. She was anxious for the train to start moving. She wanted to be alone.

She was alone now. She sat looking out the train window. She felt empty. Empty and weary. She did not care to analyze, mediate, or think now. She was satisfied to look out the window of the moving Pullman car. She could do all the weighing and wondering later. All she wanted to do now was look at the Jersey landscape.

ELEVEN

She was glad to be back. She wanted to get started on her new book. Everything else would have to wait.

On her first morning back, Mary Anne worked well for a few hours. But then it became difficult. She struggled along, hoping to work herself to an inspired period when the book would seem to write itself. She thought of writing to George but she put it off until the third morning. Then, she wrote him of her work and told him again how sorry she was that he hadn't been able to go to Paris with her.

Mary Anne was sitting at her desk near an opened window. She thought about the monotony in the repetition of emotions. Here she was, waiting for letters from George Boorstein again. These were the same doubts, the same thoughts she had experienced before while waiting for his letters. She had now worked herself into the same state that she had after her first meeting with him. But there was less intensity this time.

Perhaps when she finished this book, she would resolve her feelings toward him. In the meantime, she had to reserve her emotional strength for her work. She still tired easily.

Mary Anne Read did not think that there was anything seriously wrong with her. When she became tired, she rested. Then she would resume her work. Becoming tired once more, she rested again. She didn't bother to consult a doctor. She had been frail even as a child. That was all it was. Writing required complete concentration. It was no wonder she was tired so often. She had never been strong and she persisted in work that demanded so much. She was convinced that her condition was not something to be troubled over. She did not want to have to worry about her health.

Unconsciously, Mary Anne did worry. She didn't go to a doctor because she was afraid that he would find something seriously wrong with her. And if there were, it wouldn't do her any good to know. If not, it would have been a waste of time better spent on her book.

Mary Anne was an exceptionally intelligent young woman and she knew that she was not acting rationally. It was probably neurotic, neurasthenic. But whatever it was, sooner or later, she would get over it. She'd have to.

Four months had passed since she had blown a kiss to George Boorstein from her Pullman car in Pennsylvania Station. In that time, he had written only a few commonplace letters. He wrote nothing of a personal nature. In fact, after his second letter, he even stopped telling her that he missed her. To Mary Anne, this meant that the end had finally been reached. At times she would accept this but she never believed that the relationship was beyond rehabilitation. When this new book was written, she would take the manuscript to New York. Once they saw each other, the relationship would resume.

Mary Anne poured her energy into her writing with a new fervor. She drained herself daily and her periods of fatigue began to occur more frequently. At times, she would lie in bed, her weariness so great that the flow of her consciousness was almost stilled. Then, slowly, she would revive. As she began to feel stronger, her despondency would decrease. As she regained her strength, she would be up and on her feet, at her work.

Thus the days passed for Mary Anne.

Mary Anne Read decided to move back to Virginia. She had long since quit her job at the library. In fact, she had quit even before the completion of her first book. She could not hold down a job and write a novel. Mary Anne knew that moving would be an interruption of her work but this would be a matter of days. She would finish her book once she was settled in Virginia.

But after the move, Mary Anne was exhausted. She could not get out of her bed. Her family brought in Dr. Bell to see her. Mary Anne was relieved. It had been taken out of her hands. She was utterly and completely spent. She had neither the energy nor the will to argue when her father told her that he had telephoned Dr. Bell.

Dr. Bell came to the house, examined her, and asked many questions. Then, he suggested that she go into Richmond Hospital for tests. At the question in her eyes, he smiled, patted her as he had when she was a child: "Nothing serious, Mary Anne, I just want to run off some blood tests. I suspect you might be a little anemic. Now that you're home, we'll build you up again."

TWELVE

Mary Anne had been in bed for several weeks. She had spent two weeks in the hospital. According to Dr. Bell, her blood count was found to be so low that she had been given transfusions. At first she had been suspicious but she had to admit that she did feel better afterwards. She was getting her strength back, slowly but surely. It was foolish of her to have waited so long. She read, she slept, she translated poems by the French Symbolist poets. She wrote letters. She wrote to George telling him that she was still confined to bed but that her condition was not serious.

"By serious, read Fatal," she wrote.

She also told him that she had put aside her novel until she was stronger. But she expected to resume her work in another two or three weeks. Her letter was cordial but not personal. She sealed the envelope and addressed it. When Cora Lee came in to straighten her sheets, she noticed it and offered to mail it for her. Mary Anne smiled her thanks.

Cora Lee had been in the Read family since Mary Anne was a little girl. She was a lean, tall black woman with very dark skin. She was old and although her long shoulders were bent, her hair was still black and tightly coiled. Mary Anne watched her leaving the bedroom holding the letter to George Boorstein. She could have cried. She was touched by Cora Lee's affection. Over the years, the black woman's love for Mary Anne had made itself known. Every time Mary Anne had visited the family from Atlanta, Cora Lee would hover over her, ask her questions about her life, coax her to eat more, prepare her special favorites. Mr. and Mrs. Read were always pleased to see their only child but what they considered good taste prevented them from making the fuss over her that Cora Lee did. Cora Lee had no such inhibitions. Any favorable clipping in the newspaper would be cut out, folded and unfolded, in the grocery store, for the milk man. And since her illness, her love for Mary Anne was revealed daily through the devoted care she gave the girl. Cora Lee would not permit her to so much as lift a finger. She was supposed to rest and rest she would.

Cora Lee was worried about Mary Anne. She had reason to be. She'd overheard Mr. and Mrs. Read talking about the child. What a shame it would be if such a pretty little thing were to die so young. But then she could remember that even as a young 'un, Mary Anne had been sickly. She had never been any trouble, though. She'd sit for hours in a chair by the window watching people outdoors. Or reading her father's books. It was no wonder the child was so smart —she had done a lot of reading. But Mary Anne was more than smart; she was a good child. Nobody had ever treated her, Cora Lee, the way little Mary Anne did. She wasn't like the other Southern ladies who talk sweet to you, sweet like you're a child, or a pet, or a dummy, explaining everything more than once like you were dumb. Even after Mary Anne had grown up and moved away, she never came to see her parents without coming in to see Cora Lee, sitting down at the table with her in the kitchen to have coffee or tea and find out how Cora Lee and her family were. There was something special about Mary Anne. It would be a shame if something happened to her. God shouldn't let it. She was worried. Mary Anne just didn't look perky; her colorin' was wrong. And you didn't have to be a college graduate to know that when Dr. Bell was talking to the Reads about Mary Anne's blood count and saying something about more of one color cells than another that it was serious. Just the tone of his voice let you know he was serious. And the look on ol' Mr. Read's face.

Mary Anne was still pale but she felt much better. Dr. Bell insisted that she take it easy a while longer. Mary Anne hoped it wouldn't be too much longer. She was tired of taking it easy. Her mind was alert; she was filled with ideas. Lying in bed doing nothing was so frustrating she could scream. The next time he came in she would tell him that she wanted to get back to work.

Mary Anne didn't have to tell Dr. Bell. He told her. He told her that she could start working again provided she didn't work too hard.

Now that she was up and about, Mary Anne was not sure of herself. She didn't know how much she could do, how much effort she could make. She did not know what her limits were, what was "too hard."

Mary Anne resumed her writing in a state of uncertainty. In a few days, this uncertainty vanished. She could go on doing whatever work she wanted to do. After her long rest, she felt fresh and energetic. In fact, she felt stronger than she had in years. And once she began writing, she generated fresh enthusiasm and worked well.

Mary Anne had no other symptoms of being ill. She was back at work and making good progress. She did not worry about her health; she saw no reason to.

George wrote her a letter of congratulations. She had written telling him that she was fully recovered and that she was back at work and making progress. George's letter was friendly but definitely guarded. This hurt but not as much as it would have earlier. Her love was beginning to change into a memory of love. At times it was. At such times, the hurt was softened by sadness.

THIRTEEN

Mary Anne decided to call her second novel *Faithful Lovers Live in Caskets*. When she wrote George about the title, she anticipated the same furor that her first title had created. She sent him the manuscript.

She expected that the office would like the novel but not the title. She waited with some amusement. She enjoyed speculating about the reactions. She did not have to wait long. An envelope came with the Herzog name on it. She tore it open quickly and unfolded the letter. George had written congratulations about the novel. He and the others in the office liked the book and Herzog wanted to publish it. However, they were all in accord on the title. It should be changed. Mary Anne wrote back that she considered the title right for her novel and that she could not think of any other title for it. A correspondence ensued.

Mary Anne remained adamant.

Finally, she received a letter from George in which he stated that since she insisted upon it, they would publish her novel with the title *Faithful Lovers Live in Caskets*.

Mary Anne had expected to have her own way about the title. She was pleased to get the letter. She didn't want a long drawn-out quarrel and a lot of haggling about it.

She looked at George's signature. *Sincerely*, he had written. He had eased out of their affair and she had not stopped him. He probably thought that he was being civilized and considerate to ease out of it.

With her second novel finished, Mary Anne was at loose ends. She could go to New York but it was too soon for another New

York trip. She could go somewhere else, of course. But where?

Mary Anne was experiencing the aftermath of her love affair. Her feeling of loss was like that which rises out of the passage of time. The affair had been frustrating from the beginning. George Boorstein simply did not have a gift for expressing his feelings. She had known this from the start. She had also known that George was primarily a businessman. She had willfully ignored all that she knew and acted against her judgment. In fact, when she thought of it, she was lucky. She had caused herself some unhappiness but it could have been worse.

There was such a feeling of emptiness now. It must be the combination of the two endings—the ending of her affair and the ending of her novel. But was it really? She had published three books. They were all fine books, she knew this. She was still a young woman; and she was holding her own insofar as her health was concerned. She would write more. She wanted to do the LaForgue translations.

She knew that men were attracted to her but she hadn't done much by way of looking for one. She could have created opportunities but she hadn't. And now she missed having a man. She had always assumed there would be a man in her life—either as a lover or a husband. She had never felt that marriage was a necessity because she didn't want children. In spite of her background, Mary Anne never berated herself for not wanting to have children. Hers was a justified selfishness. She had to use her strength selectively. She could not pursue her writing and raise a family. Some women could but she wasn't strong enough. With her, it had to be one or the other and she had no difficulty in making the decision. She had never seriously wanted children or marriage, not since she began to have her own consciousness of the world rather than the conventional views of society. She had never seriously contemplated having children although she was curious about the experience of motherhood. She was still curious but her health would not permit her to go through such an ordeal unless she were to sacrifice her literary career. And this she would not do.

On this day, then, her life was empty. And yet, it was within her power to create a whole world to fill her life. She could start another novel, a novel dealing with time. Or write a story about an artist who died young. She was too tired; she had just finished a major work. She could not muster the will power and the drive to start a new novel yet. But time was limited; she could not take time to rest. Neither could she force it. She would have to let the idea germinate. She would busy herself translating the poetry of Jules LaForgue.

Mary Anne soon became absorbed in the translations. She discovered that she could not work for as long as she had in the past. Her long rest made it seem that she had recovered but now she realized that she had not. Her mind and her will were prisoners of her body. At times she wanted to cry out against the frailty of living flesh. Death was an indignity. Whenever she thought of it, her pride was wounded. The very thought of it was an offense. Death destroyed everything that counted in a human being. It was the supreme, total, and absolute indignity. But the artist could speak after death. This was a triumph. It was not the only triumph over death but it was the greatest one.

Why was she thinking of death? She must live in order to write more books. She had not reached her peak; she had so much more to say.

Mary Anne became sad. Her metaphorical heart was too big for her physical heart.

Mary Anne decided not to go to New York for the publication of her second book. It was too much of a risk. There were so many things she could do there. She could go shopping. Walk through Central Park. Take a ferry to Hoboken. Sit in Washington Square. There were so many little things that she could have enjoyed. But the trip would tire her too much.

Mary Anne was giving up part of her life with the hope that she would have a longer life. But she could not help but want the things that she gave up. She started to look at things, at characters and events, differently. She thought of George Boorstein. His letters had become even more commonplace and literal. He was protecting himself, of course. She was certain of this. He was guarding against a renewal of any relationship with her. But why should he feel he had to? How dare he treat her as though she were one of those troublesome undignified women who became nuisances when they were no longer wanted? Didn't he know her? Hadn't their relationship given him any insight as to what she was?

As indignant as she felt at times, as exasperated as his letters left her, each one opened up hope in her as she ripped the envelope. Her love for George Boorstein was an outlived love that could not be restored. But battered and outlived, it remained. Love was neither reasonable nor rational. Love had its own doomed logical illogic. It could be imperious in its demands. George Boorstein was not the kind of man she had expected to love. He was dull most of the time. And he was a Jew. She had never made any attempt to probe into her own self as to why she had found him attractive but she had understood, as had he, that the fact that he was a Jew had much to do with her love for him. She had been attracted to him without any thought of what he was. It was not until after they had become lovers that she had given thought to his being a Jew. And at the time, this had added to his physical attraction. Sleeping somewhere in her must have been the notion that a Jew was more sensual.

Be all this as it may, she had soon learned that George Boorstein was an American businessman first. This was not altered by the fact that he was a Jew. His attractiveness had not waned. Mary Anne had merely pushed this fact into a dormant state.

Their affair was over but she loved him. This was beyond her will and decision. Whatever he was, she loved him. Against her better judgment, she loved him. In spite of the fact that it was over, she loved him.

And she had lost him.

FOURTEEN

The reviews of *Faithful Lovers Live in Caskets* were disappointing. Sunday papers across the country carried news of the book's publication. Some said that *Faithful Lovers Live in Caskets* was a novel without ideals. Others wrote that *Faithful Lovers* was merely a repetition of *The Morning after the Honeymoon*. And there were those who said that Mary Anne Read could not write. One reviewer said that her technique and style were interesting but that she had nothing to say. H. L. Mencken hailed the book but he stood alone.

FIFTEEN

On Monday morning, sitting at his desk, George Boorstein went over some of the reviews that had been gathered for him during the preceding week. It didn't look good. Not for Mary Anne. He couldn't help but feel sorry for her. Of course, his commitment, that is to say the commitment of the Lemuel Herzog Publishing Company had ended with the publication of this novel. If she were in fact written out, they could cut their losses immediately. But it wouldn't be so easy for Mary Anne. With all her charm and attractiveness, no one but a fool could miss seeing that writing was her life. Everything else had to fall in line after her work.

He looked at the reviews again. More would be coming in. There might be some favorable ones. Of course, Mencken's would carry weight. But the rest had all but ganged up on her. He had seen this happen before. There was no accounting for it. How would Mary Anne react to it? He would wait until some more reviews came in and then he would write her. He couldn't give her too much encouragement, not as an editor. But as a friend, he might.

Cora Lee walked out the back door. She would pick a flower to put on Mary Anne's tray this morning. She hadn't been eating right lately. And she was sleeping more every day. She had heard Dr. Bell say that she might have to go back to the hospital again. Mrs. Read had told Dr. Bell that it could be that Mary Anne was just upset because of what people were saying about her new book. Cora Lee smiled. Some women didn't even know their own children. Cora Lee had watched Mary Anne reading some of the notices. Sometimes she had laughed. She explained it all to Cora Lee.

She told her that there were some folks who lived off other folks. Someone would sit down and write a book. Then these other folks would read it and tell people whether or not they should buy it. They spent a lot of time copying each other because they were all scared that they might like or not like the wrong book. Mary Anne told her that most writers did not let these folks bother them. It did bother them sometimes because the big publishers in New York sometimes got scared off and wouldn't want to print your books if they all had said they didn't like your last one. This was the only problem and even though it could be serious, most writers went on writing.

Cora Lee could tell Mrs. Read right now that her child didn't give a hoot what those people were writing about her new book. She was going to write another book, a big one. Mary Anne had already told her this.

There, that was a pretty flower. Mary Anne would like that one. She always had an eye for pretty things, Mary Anne did. She wouldn't be able to resist her breakfast this morning. It would look as good as it would taste.

Balancing the tray on her left hand, she knocked on Mary Anne's door. There was no answer. With a grave sense of misgiving, Cora Lee opened the door. She knew, even before she drew back the blinds, that her Mary Anne was dead.